TOO MANY JOBS!

Stevie stared at the calendar in shock.

"What's the problem?" Carole asked.

"The fourth weekend of the month," Stevie said. "It's less than three weeks away."

"Right, so—"

"The end of the month is when the hospital festival takes place," Lisa explained.

"Oh, no," Carole said.

"And that's not all," Stevie said, getting her voice back. "It includes the day of the twenty-eighth."

"So what momentous event happens on the twenty-eighth?" Carole's father asked.

"Debates for president of the Middle School," Stevie informed him.

"My dear," he said. "If you can handle all of these things at once, you don't need to worry about becoming president of the Middle School. You'll be qualified to be president of the United States!"

"If," Stevie said ominously.

THE SADDLE CLUB

TEAM PLAY

BONNIE BRYANT

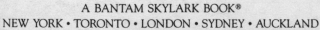

A BANTAM SKYLARK BOOK®
NEW YORK · TORONTO · LONDON · SYDNEY · AUCKLAND

RL 5, 009–012

TEAM PLAY
A Bantam Skylark Book / March 1991

ISBN 0-553-15862-7

Published simultaneously in the United States and Canada

PRINTED IN THE UNITED STATES OF AMERICA

OPM   0 9 8 7 6 5 4 3 2 1

For Ginee Seo

"IF YOU'RE GETTING some hay, can you bring me a flake?"
Stevie Lake asked her best friend Carole Hanson. They
were in the stalls at Pine Hollow Stables, where they rode
horses and took lessons. Class was over and it was time to
groom and feed their horses.

"Oh, sure," Carole said. "There's a bale right here."
She leaned over, took a handful of hay, and gave it to
Stevie.

Stevie loosened the stalks of hay and put it into Topside's manger. The horse tugged some strands out with
his teeth, worked them into his mouth with his soft
lips, and munched contentedly as Stevie continued the
grooming. When his coat was shiny, she patted him ad-
miringly. He lifted his head from his manger, glanced at

her as if to give her a hurried thanks, and returned his attention to the food in front of him.

Stevie smiled. Taking care of horses was *almost* as much fun as riding them.

"Almost done?" Lisa Atwood asked. Stevie nodded. Lisa was Stevie's other best friend. Along with Carole, the three of them had formed a group called The Saddle Club. It was a club with only two rules: All the members had to be horse crazy and they had to be willing to help one another. The first rule was easy. The second rule sometimes led to a lot of work, but as long as it had to do with friends and horses, the work usually seemed like fun.

"Max said he wants to see the whole class in his office after all the chores are done," Lisa told Stevie. "I'll go see who needs help."

Stevie grinned. "Isn't it funny how everything Max wants is always 'after all the chores are done'?"

Lisa laughed. Max was the owner of Pine Hollow and a firm believer in horse care as well as horse riding. All of his riders spent a lot of time caring for their horses. They knew that horse care was important, and having riders care for their horses kept costs down at the stables. There were a lot of kids whose parents couldn't have afforded lessons if that meant also paying for extra Pine Hollow stable hands.

"Well, I'm going to go help Anna," Lisa said. "She

rode Patch today and he got a lot of mud on him. She's going to hose him down. I'm his shampoo girl. See you later."

"Okay. I'll come help when I'm done," Stevie said. She picked up a bucket and headed for the supply area where she could get some fresh wood chips for bedding. She filled her bucket and lugged it back to the stall, running through a mental checklist as she walked quickly along the aisle of the stable.

Let's see, she thought. *Stow the tack, give him water, clean the stall, pick his hooves, curry his coat, brush it, brush his mane and tail—I have to do all that and then—*

"—Oooof!" Stevie exclaimed, tripping over something and landing flat on her stomach. The wood chips flew out of the bucket and scattered all over the floor.

"Oh, good," Veronica diAngelo's sweet, insincere voice said. "The floor here needed some fresh chips. Thank you, Stevie."

Veronica was Pine Hollow's spoiled little rich girl and The Saddle Club's least favorite person. Unlike the other riders, she never did any work if she could help it.

Stevie rose slowly, knowing nothing was damaged except her patience, never her strongest trait anyway. She looked to see what had tripped her. It was a pitchfork that Veronica had left on the floor. Pitchforks could be dangerous! Stevie glared at Veronica for her carelessness.

"Too bad something got in your way," Veronica said.

"You know, the same sort of thing happened to me in class today, when somebody pulled their horse ahead of mine and made her shy."

Stevie recalled the incident. Veronica and her horse, Garnet, were in front of her and Topside. As usual, Veronica was having difficulty controlling Garnet. Since they were cantering in circles and there was clearly room to pass, Stevie had simply passed Veronica. But Topside had been pretty irritated with the situation, and in spite of Stevie's genuine effort to control him, he'd cut right in front of Garnet, kicking dirt in the mare's face. Not surprisingly, Garnet had shied. It had taken Veronica a few minutes to get her back under control. Stevie had felt a little bad about that. It was bad riding form. But if Veronica had controlled her horse properly in the first place, she never would have had the trouble.

Stevie started to try to explain to Veronica, but there wasn't much point in it. Veronica wasn't the listening type. She wasn't interested in anybody but herself.

"Here's your pitchfork," Stevie said, finally rising to her feet. She handed it to Veronica.

"Oh, I guess this *is* mine," she said, pretending to look surprised. "I wondered what someone had done with it," she added vaguely.

That was when Stevie realized that Veronica had put it on the floor on purpose. The girl was unbelievably mean—or stupid—or both.

4

Stevie promised herself she'd get even, but not right then. Right then, she had a bucket to refill and a horse to care for.

When she returned with a fresh bucket full of wood chips, she found Max standing by Garnet's stable, talking to Veronica and a young girl whom she'd never seen before. Stevie ducked into Topside's stall, spread the wood chips, and listened.

"Veronica, this is Melanie," Max said. "She's going to be taking a lesson in about twenty minutes. I'd like you to show her around and help her saddle up one of the ponies for her first lesson. Let's put her on Quarter, okay?"

Veronica glared at Max. Everybody knew that one of the chores Max expected his riders to perform was to show new riders the ropes. Inside her stall, Stevie stifled a snort of disbelief. She'd love to see Veronica do anything, let alone teach a new rider!

"And Veronica, when you're done helping Melanie, you can come to the meeting in my office," Max continued. "It'll start in about fifteen minutes. Bring Melanie along, will you?"

"Sure, Max," Veronica said. As soon as he left, she turned her back on Melanie and began hugging Garnet.

"That's a really pretty horse," Melanie said.

"Of course she is," Veronica responded. "She's a purebred Arabian. She's mine, you know."

"Your very own?" The awe was clear in the younger girl's voice. "Do you take care of her all by yourself?" Melanie asked.

"Yes," Veronica replied. "And it's a lot of work."

Stevie could hardly believe what she was hearing. Veronica's idea of a lot of work was putting the pitchfork where somebody was going to trip on it!

"How did you learn it all?" Melanie asked.

Stevie wanted to hear the answer to that one, too, because as nearly as she could tell, Veronica hadn't learned *any* of it yet!

"Oh, you'll see," Veronica said.

Melanie probably will, Stevie thought. *She'll see what a lazy, spoiled, good-for-nothing, bratty—*

"Oh, Re—ed!" Veronica called out sweetly. Red was Red O'Malley, Pine Hollow's chief stable hand and occasional instructor. Veronica tended to view him as her personal groom.

"Yes, Veronica," he said, sighing as he spoke. He knew he was about to be given a job Veronica was supposed to do herself.

"Would you please saddle up Quarter for this girl, uh, Melodie?"

"Melanie," Stevie called out over her stall, surprising Veronica. Veronica had apparently forgotten how close Topside's stall was and that Stevie could overhear everything.

"Whatever," Veronica said airily, undisturbed by her own rudeness.

Stevie stuck her head out of Topside's stall and gestured to the little girl. "Come on, Melanie. I'll introduce you to Quarter and show you how to tack him up."

"Thanks, Stevie," Red said gratefully.

Veronica said nothing.

It only took Stevie a few minutes to put a saddle and bridle on Quarter. The look of delighted anticipation on Melanie's face was worth every bit of the work.

"Will I really be able to do that myself?" she asked.

Stevie smiled as she nodded. Melanie reminded her of herself when she first began riding at about the same age. Everything had seemed so wonderfully mysterious. She thought Veronica was really missing something by not doing her own work and not helping others. As far as Veronica was concerned, though, it was clear that "work" was something you got somebody else to do.

"Time for the meeting in Max's office. Then you'll be able to ride," Stevie said. The two girls left Quarter's stall, closed the door, latched it tightly, and headed for Max's spacious office, where all the young riders were gathered.

A puzzled look crossed Max's face when he saw Stevie come in with Melanie. Veronica was already seated comfortably in the one soft chair in his office. Then Stevie saw him nod to himself and she knew that he realized

7

exactly what had happened. No matter how many times Max asked Veronica to do something, she always seemed to find a way to get somebody else to do it.

Stevie and Melanie sat on the floor next to Carole and Lisa, where they had saved a space for her. Carole glanced at Melanie and gave Stevie a questioning look. "Veronica," Stevie whispered. It was all the explanation that was needed. Carole nodded and whispered to Lisa.

Max cleared his throat. "This is just a quick announcement," he began. "But I think it's a rather exciting one. Pine Hollow has just become involved with an international exchange program, and as our first part of that program, we will be welcoming some guests here in three weeks. An Italian equestrian team will be staying with me for a few days. During that time, they will perform for all of our riders and will give instruction in certain techniques that they have been working on. I know we'll enjoy having them here and I know we'll learn a lot from them. I also know that you will all welcome them and give them help whenever needed. Let me say right now that this is not a small job. This team is going to need a lot of help during their stay."

Stevie looked over at Veronica. "And you know, for some of us, 'help' is our middle name," she blurted out. There was silence for a few seconds. Then almost everybody began laughing. Everybody knew exactly who

Stevie meant. Even Max seemed to be stifling a grin. Veronica just glared at Stevie.

"What I really want to do today is to find a volunteer," Max continued. "I need one person who will be able to spend time with these four boys."

Stevie could have sworn that Veronica sat up straighter when Max said the word "boys."

"My volunteer will show them around the stable, show them around the town and generally act as a host for them when they are not with me. Any volunteers?"

Veronica's hand shot up.

Stevie's heart sank. She could just imagine the kind of tour Veronica would give to four Italian boys and the kind of help they'd get. But Veronica was eager as could be, waving her hand in Max's face.

It was more than Stevie could take. "Oh Re–ed," she mimicked. "Saddle up these boys' horses, will you? *After* you've cleaned Garnet's stall?"

The laughter was louder this time.

"So you're volunteering, Stevie?" Max asked.

"I am?"

"That's great. I know you'll do a wonderful job. Thank you, Stevie," Max said. "Okay, class as usual on Tuesday."

That was a dismissal.

"Saddle Club meeting at TD's in ten minutes," Lisa said.

"Five," Carole said pointedly.

"Let's go," Stevie agreed, patting her pocket to see if she had any money for a sundae. "Uh-oh, I'm out of money," she complained.

"And that's not all you're out of!" Carole said.

Lisa put her arm across Stevie's shoulder. "Yeah, pal. You're out of your head, too."

"I didn't volunteer!" Stevie protested. "Max roped me into it."

"That's not what's going to get you in the worst trouble," Carole began, walking on Stevie's other side. "Making fun of Veronica in front of practically the whole world can be a really bad mistake."

"Oh, who cares about spoiled brat Veronica di-Angelo?" Stevie asked with disgust.

Carole and Lisa looked at one another. Stevie had a lot to learn!

THE THREE GIRLS walked together toward Willow Creek's little shopping center, the home of their favorite hangout, Tastee Delight. It was an ice-cream shop better known to them as TD's, and the site of a lot of their Saddle Club meetings. One of the advantages of having a club with almost no rules was that they could have meetings any place they wanted, whenever they wanted.

Lisa found a booth in the back where at least one of them could watch the door in case Veronica arrived, seeking revenge.

"Now, down to business," Lisa began, taking the seat which faced the door.

Just then a waitress approached the trio. "Oh, no. It's *you*," she said, looking at Stevie. Stevie was famous for ordering ridiculous combinations of ice cream. Her friends suspected she did it so nobody would want tastes of her order.

"Don't worry," Stevie assured the waitress. "I'm out of money. I'll just have a glass of water."

The waitress sighed with relief.

"Oh, I'll pay for you," Lisa said. "Have whatever you want."

"Really?" Stevie asked. Lisa nodded. "Okay, then, in honor of my new Italian connection, I'll have some spumoni—"

The waitress wrote that down and turned to Lisa. But Stevie wasn't finished yet.

"—with some pineapple topping," Stevie continued. The woman wrote it down quickly. "And have you got some walnuts—you know, the syrupy ones?" The woman nodded weakly. "And coconut sprinkles. With a cherry, of course."

The woman dashed away.

"Did you guys want something?" Stevie asked, pretending she had no idea about why the woman ran away.

"She'll bring us the usual normal sundaes," Carole said. "At this table, those stand out, you know."

"Now, down to business," Lisa said pointedly. "What made you get into a fight with Veronica?"

"Everything always makes me get into a fight with Veronica," Stevie said. "She's the most awful girl I know.

She thinks that just because she's got pots of money, she should have everything else, too. But life isn't like that and sometimes I just feel I have to point it out to her. Know what I mean?"

"Well, sure," Lisa said. "We all feel that way. The only difference is that we try not to act on those feelings. Do you have any idea how vindictive Veronica is?"

"Vindictive?" Stevie echoed. She was a little irritated that Lisa used a word she didn't know, but Lisa was a straight-A student and straight-A students sometimes did things like that.

"Vindictive means she's going to get revenge," Carole explained. Carole shrugged at Stevie's look of surprise. "Revenge is a big Marine Corps subject," she explained, smiling wryly. Her father was a colonel in the Marine Corps and Carole had been raised on Marine bases around the country. Lisa and Stevie both smiled at the remark.

"Come on. What can Veronica do to me?" Stevie asked.

"I don't know," Lisa said. "But whatever it is, she'll try it. Count on it!"

"Well, I call for a change of subject," Stevie said. She was getting tired of listening to her friends' warnings.

"All right, I've got a new one," Carole said. "What's Phil Marston going to think about you escorting four handsome Italian boys around town while they're here?"

Phil was Stevie's boyfriend. They had met the summer before at riding camp. He lived in a nearby town, and although they only saw one another about once a month, they talked every week.

"This doesn't have anything to do with Phil," Stevie said. "And besides, it means you guys will have four handsome, probably rich, and dashing Italian boys to share. You know as well as I do that Max didn't just volunteer me, he volunteered you, too."

The waitress arrived, holding her tray high. "One hot fudge on vanilla." She put it in front of Lisa. "One caramel on vanilla." Carole got that. "And one, uh—oh, I can't even say it." She slammed the dish down in front of Stevie and dashed away.

"I can't think what comes over that woman!" Stevie said. "Isn't she just the silliest?" She picked up her spoon and then asked politely, "Anybody want a taste?"

"No, thanks," Lisa and Carole said at the same time.

Lisa continued, "You mean you think hosting this Italian equestrian team is some sort of Saddle Club project? That Carole and I are going to have to pitch in and spend a lot of time with these handsome, dashing, rich, talented Italian boys?"

"That's exactly what I had in mind." Stevie grinned proudly.

"I wonder how good they are at riding," Carole said. Although all three of them were certifiably horse crazy,

Carole was the horse craziest of the bunch. She had long ago decided that horses would be her life. She hadn't decided whether she was going to train, ride, raise, or heal them, but it would be one or all of them, of that she was certain. "I mean, I wonder if they're as good as Kate Devine," she mused.

Kate Devine was an out-of-town member of The Saddle Club. Her parents owned a dude ranch in the southwest which The Saddle Club had already visited twice, and hoped to visit again in the future. Before moving to the ranch and taking up Western riding, Kate had been a championship English rider. She'd helped The Saddle Club girls with both kinds of riding. In turn, they had helped her remember how much fun riding could be when she'd given it up because she'd stopped enjoying competing.

"Wouldn't it be neat if these guys were going near Kate's ranch and she could see them, too?" Lisa asked.

Stevie grinned. "Somehow I don't see these boys traveling into cowboy country with their dressage show, do you?"

"No, I guess not," Lisa agreed. "It was just an—uh-oh."

Lisa's "uh-oh" could only mean one thing.

"Ah, the winner of the Helping Hand Award has arrived?" Stevie said sarcastically. Lisa nodded. Veronica sauntered in, looked disparagingly at The Saddle Club, and chose a table as far away from them as she could get. "Wow, I just got a neat idea," Stevie said excitedly, leaning forward and whispering to her friends. Lisa and Carole had learned from past experience that Stevie's neat ideas were usually wonderful, and often got them all into a lot of trouble. They suspected this time would be no exception.

Stevie signaled the waitress and explained what she wanted. The poor woman gawked in horror and shook her head, but agreed to do as Stevie asked.

"I think we'd better get out of here," Stevie said. Lisa and Carole agreed that that was the wisest move.

As they were leaving, the beleaguered waitress was delivering an order to Veronica.

"That one," she said, pointing to Stevie, "she says she owes you an apology or something. Wanted you to have this sundae. She paid for it. It's just like the one she had, too."

"Oh, really?" Veronica asked. Stevie could see a smug look of victory cross her face. Veronica thought she'd won. "What is it?"

The waitress's face paled. "It's spumoni," she began. "With pineapple, walnuts, coconut—" She couldn't finish, however. Veronica was already shrieking.

3

ALL SUNDAY AFTERNOON, when she should have been starting her homework, Stevie worked on a list of things to show the Italian boys, places of interest in town, places of interest at the stable. She planned a full-scale tour of Washington, D.C., because, after all, it was only about forty-five minutes away. Stevie did notice that her list encompassed activities that would take a determined person a few months rather than a few days to accomplish. But, she told herself, at least the boys would have some choices.

She also borrowed an Italian phrase book from the library and spent all of Sunday evening, when she should have been finishing her homework, making a list of words and phrases she thought she might need to know. That included everything from "horseback riding" (*a cavallo*) to "Can you repair a flat tire?" (*Può riparare una gomma a terra?*), although she wasn't quite sure how she would work the last phrase into a conversation. The end result of all her work was that she was up way too late on Sunday, finishing the homework she should have done much earlier, and overslept on Monday morning.

Stevie fairly flew out of bed when she saw what time it was. She pulled on her clothes, hoping, as an afterthought, that she hadn't put on her sweater backwards, and dashed downstairs and out the door, grabbing a doughnut from the kitchen counter as she raced through the room.

"Glad to see you eating a balanced breakfast!" her mother called after her. Stevie couldn't answer. Her mouth was full of doughnut by then.

Stevie went to a different school from the one Lisa and Carole went to. She went to Fenton Hall, which was a private school in town. Lisa and Carole both went to Willow Creek's public school. Stevie had been at Fenton Hall ever since kindergarten and she liked it, although she would have loved to see Lisa and Carole every day, not just on riding days. But Fenton Hall was good, as schools went. Its only major drawback was that Veronica diAngelo went there, too, and was in some of Stevie's classes.

None of this was on Stevie's mind as she walked

quickly to school. She was thinking about all the work she'd done to prepare for the Italian boys' visit. She pulled one of her lists out of her pocket and admired the plans she'd written there for them. People often accused Stevie of hurrying through work and not being thorough. But this list was nothing if not thorough! Stevie was very pleased with herself. It occurred to her that she might be turning over a new leaf. She liked the feeling of being prepared. She liked knowing that she was helping others. In a small way, she was doing something that was going to make a difference, and she felt good about it.

Then she looked at her watch and didn't feel quite so good. Mondays always began with a school-wide assembly and she'd missed it. All of it. With a bit of luck, she might be able to mingle with the crowd returning to her classroom. If it weren't for the fact that she was still wearing her jacket, she might even be able to mingle right into her first class without anyone noticing. Maybe Miss Epworth hadn't taken roll yet.

"Hey, congratulations on your new job!" one of her classmates greeted her in the hallway.

Stevie smiled and nodded and tried to look inconspicuous. News got around fast at a small school like Fenton. Quite a few of Pine Hollow's riders went there. Stevie figured one of them must have told some of the other students about the Italian boys.

"You're going to be great," Patty Featherstone said,

clapping Stevie on the back. Stevie didn't think Patty Featherstone had ever clapped her on the back before. She wouldn't mind if she never did it again, either. Stevie's shoulder smarted from Patty's enthusiasm.

Stevie followed a group of students into her classroom, slipping out of her jacket on the way. She slid it into her book bag and tried to look as if she'd been at school for a long time.

"Oh, Stevie, how nice to have you join us," Miss Epworth greeted her. *So much for that idea,* Stevie thought. Then she wondered why Miss Epworth didn't seem angry.

By fourth period, Stevie began to smell a rat. The third person to congratulate her that morning also mentioned that it was Veronica who had told them the news. Stevie was sure that Veronica would never do anything nice to her. Therefore, this news that Veronica was telling everyone had to be something bad. So, then, why was everybody congratulating her and clapping her on the back?

Stevie found out at lunchtime. She was about to bite into the school cook's version of pizza when the P.A. system called her and told her to report to the principal's office.

Stevie could think of dozens of reasons why the principal might want to see her, up to and including being a half hour late this morning. What she couldn't figure out was how the principal had heard about those dozen things, and why it was that wherever she'd been all morning, people had kept clapping her on the back.

"You wanted to see me, Miss Fenton?" Stevie asked.

"Oh, yes! Good, come on in, Stevie." It was the first time she'd ever seen Miss Fenton smile and call her Stevie. Something was definitely wrong with the world today. Stevie came in and sat down.

"My dear," she began. "You have agreed to take on an important task and responsibility."

Stevie was about to reach for her lists. She wanted to show Miss Fenton that she'd really already done most of the work.

"What you are doing can make an enormous difference to these youngsters."

Enormous? Really, what's the big deal here? Stevie thought.

"The hospital counts on Fenton Hall students to show the young patients a good time for one afternoon. Frankly, Stevie, when I learned it was you who had volunteered to chair the event this year, I was pleased. You're not the best student in the school, but you do show a certain, shall I say, genius, when it comes to amusement—though there have been times . . . No, I won't go into that now. In any event, dear, I am confident that you will use that genius to give the hospital patients a wonderful time at the annual festival at the end of this month."

Stevie couldn't believe what she was hearing. If she got it right, Miss Fenton was under the impression that she had volunteered to be the chairman of the school's annual Children's Hospital Festival. That meant taking the kids in the hospital for wheelchair rides. Stevie had been one of the pushers one year. The kids had been bored to tears.

"Often, I'm afraid," Miss Fenton continued, "our student volunteers have been rather unimaginative when it came to entertaining the young hospital patients. With you at the helm, Stevie, I'm *sure* those days are past."

"Oh." It was all Stevie could think of to say. Her mind was scanning every second of every day of the last week, trying to remember exactly when it was that she had volunteered for this particular job. Her thoughts were interrupted by Miss Fenton.

"On your way out, Miss Ward will give you some material on the hospital, the name and number of the person to call there, and information on what has been done in previous years. Good luck, dear."

Stevie went to Miss Ward's desk, took the material, and returned to the lunchroom and her lunch.

Her classmates had all finished their lunches and had escaped to the gym until next period, which was in ten minutes. Stevie was almost alone. It gave her time to think of the astonishing events of the day so far.

It was unusual for everybody to be so nice to her. She wasn't crazy about being clapped on the back, but it was nice to have people think good things about her. Weird as Miss Fenton was—and that was pretty weird—it was nice that she'd been so confident that Stevie would do a better job with the hospital festival than had ever been done before. The Festival had been as dull as could be in the past. Stevie probably *could* do a better job. In fact, she decided, she *would.* There were a lot of kids in Children's Hospital who could stand to have some fun, a really good time. It must be terrible to have people constantly stick them with needles and do tests on them and make them take medicine. Maybe Stevie and her schoolmates couldn't heal them, but there was no reason why they couldn't give them a good time.

Stevie smiled to herself. She'd done most of the work she would need to do for the Italian boys last night. How much more work could this be? All she had to do was to think of something fun, arrange it with the hospital, and she'd be done. And she'd feel even better about herself. Stevie realized that she was a lucky person. She had all kinds of resources, including her imagination. With a little bit of effort, she could share those resources and actually make a difference in somebody else's life. It didn't matter whether that somebody else was an Italian rider or an American hospital patient. Stevie could help.

She was definitely turning over a new leaf.

STEVIE COULD HARDLY wait to share her news with her friends. She had gotten the most wonderful idea about using horses for the Children's Hospital Festival. Although the festival was a Fenton Hall project, Stevie would never do anything with horses without consulting Lisa and Carole, too.

As soon as she got home, she dashed for the phone. There was no answer at Carole's house, and she got an answering machine when she called Lisa. Stevie thought for a minute. It was very likely that her friends were both at Pine Hollow. Since they went to the same school, they'd probably walked over to the stable together. Pine Hollow was a short walk from Stevie's house. It was an even shorter bike ride. She borrowed her twin brother

Alex's bike—hers had a broken chain—and headed for the stable.

As she had suspected, Carole and Lisa were in the outdoor schooling ring, working with Carole's horse, Starlight.

"Hi, guys!" Stevie greeted her friends.

"Oh, great!" Lisa called back from her perch on the wooden fence around the ring. "Come see what Carole's doing—and explain it to me!" she joked. Lisa had begun riding fairly recently, and though her progress had been impressive, there was still a lot she didn't know.

Stevie rode the bike up to the fence, hopped off, and propped it against the railing. She climbed up on the slats and sat next to Lisa, waving to Carole once she had gotten her balance.

Carole was standing in the middle of the ring and had Starlight on what looked like a long, flat leash. He was trotting clockwise in a large circle while Carole was turning and guiding him with a long-handled whip. Carole held his lead in her right hand and the whip with her left. She concentrated totally on what she was doing and hardly seemed aware that Stevie had arrived.

"That leash thing is a lunge line," Stevie said.

"I know that," Lisa said. "And I also know that the poles on the ground are cavallettis. What I don't know is what she's doing with them."

"Hmmm. Let me watch for a bit," Stevie said.

Carole had laid six cavallettis on the ground on one side of the ring. As Starlight trotted around the ring, he had to trot over them. They were spaced a little further apart than the natural length of his trot up until the time he reached them. Starlight had to make an effort to make his strides land between the cavallettis. When he did that, his trot was smoother and more balanced.

"She's teaching him to lengthen his strides," Stevie said. "Watch what happens after he passes the cavallettis."

The next time around, when Starlight got to the cavallettis, he adjusted his stride with less apparent effort than before and cleared them evenly. After he'd gone through all six, his stride remained long and smooth for eight or ten strides before it shortened again, reverting to his natural stride.

"It looks like he remembers for halfway around and then forgets again," Lisa observed.

"That's exactly what it is," Stevie said. "The idea is that if she keeps him going around and around, eventually he'll learn that it's easier on him to keep the long sleek stride. When that happens, he will have learned to lengthen his stride."

"Very clever," Lisa said. "So once again, the lesson is that when you're teaching a horse something, you have to repeat it and repeat it and repeat it, and eventually it sinks in."

"That's the way it is with horses," Stevie said. "And when they get it, they've got it for life."

"Hi, Stevie. I didn't see you get here," Carole said, bringing Starlight to a cooling walk. Stevie patted the forehead of the bay gelding when he drew to a stop next to her and Lisa.

"Well, when I got home, I tried to call you guys and when nobody answered, I had a feeling I'd find you here," Stevie explained.

As she stroked the horse's soft cheek, she found that some of his mane had gotten a little tangled in his bridle. Automatically, she began untangling it.

"The lesson looked pretty good," Stevie commented as she worked. "He's learning, isn't he?"

"He is," Carole said. "But it can be pretty frustrating sometimes. I know he's working hard and he wants to please me, but sometimes it seems like it takes forever! Tomorrow I think I'll try the same thing again, only riding him. Maybe I can get him to maintain the longer stride all the way around."

"Can I try lunging him?" Stevie asked.

"Sure," Carole said. "Have you ever lunged a horse before?"

"No, but I've seen it done lots of times."

Carole nodded. "Go for it."

Stevie hopped down from the fence and took Starlight's lunge line. She walked out to the middle of the ring, put the lead in her left hand, the whip in her right, and began walking him in a small circle around her in a counterclockwise direction. As he got the idea, she lengthened the lunge line and the circle became bigger. When she thought the circle was large enough, she gave Starlight a verbal command.

"Trot!" she said. He did.

"Look at that!" a new voice called from the far side of the fence. It was Veronica. "Whenever anybody needs a hand, there Stevie is, ready to pitch in! She's really something, isn't she? Your friends must be very proud of you, Stevie. I know all of Fenton Hall is." With that, she walked back into the stable.

"Good job, Stevie. Time to walk him now and let him stop for the day," Carole said, joining her friend in the center of the ring. "And time to tell me what that was all about."

Stevie told Starlight to walk and shortened the lunge line. When Lisa also reached them in the schooling ring, Stevie told them about her day.

". . . It's hard to believe all the things that are happening," she finished, "but you know what? I'm really excited. I've always thought the hospital festival was boring and today I found out that it always *has* been boring. But Miss Fenton is sure I can make it more interesting."

"You always have a way of making everything more interesting," Lisa said. "But how are you going to do it this time?"

Stevie's eyes gleamed. "I'm not sure, you know, but I'm getting this idea, and you two can help me. See—"

"Oh, Stevie!" Max called. "I just called you at home. I want to talk to you for a minute, but I think your brother, Alex, wants to talk to you even more. Something about a bike?"

Stevie looked sheepishly at Alex's bike propped up against the fence. "Mine's broken," she explained to her friends.

"Anyway, come on in here, will you?" Max asked.

Stevie handed Starlight's lunge line to Carole. "I'll see you in a few minutes." She headed for Max's office.

Veronica stopped her on her way. "Stevie," she said, and Stevie steeled herself for something unpleasant. She was surprised at Veronica's next words. "I just wanted to tell you that I admire you. You seem to be able to take on a lot without any worry. I know you'll do a good job. If there's anything I can do to help, just let me know, okay?"

Before Stevie could respond—and it would have been a long time before she could have said anything—Veronica turned and walked away into the tackroom.

Stevie thought about it as she walked to Max's office.

What was the big deal here? After all, she was just going to be a friend to some boys and she had only committed herself to spending an afternoon doing something fun with some kids in the hospital. Why would Veronica want to be part of that? She was hardly the charitable type. Before Stevie could answer her own question, she arrived at her destination.

"At your service, Max," Stevie announced, entering his office and taking a chair.

"I got the final schedule for the boys' visit," Max began. He consulted a piece of paper. "They get here on Thursday and leave late on Sunday. They will do one demonstration ride on Saturday and one on Sunday. I'd like you to think about what kinds of things you think would be fun and interesting for them to do. Then we can talk about it next week."

"We don't have to wait, Max," Stevie said. "I've already thought about it and I made a list last night." Stevie reached for the list in her back pocket, noting with pleasure the look of surprise on Max's face.

"Here it is," she said.

Max glanced at the list. He nodded. "This will do fine for the first six months of their visit, Stevie," he said solemnly, returning it to her.

"I know, I know," Stevie admitted. "There's lots more there than they could possibly do, but I just thought they might like some choices, you know?"

"I know. And it's okay. I think, however, that you can remove the tobogganing and the water slide from the list. I doubt we'll have snow at this time of year, and I'm pretty certain it won't be warm enough to swim."

"Maybe they'd just like to see them?" Stevie suggested.

"Maybe they'd rather see the Washington Monument."

"I guess." Stevie was a little hurt that Max had complaints about her list.

"Don't be upset," he said quickly. "You've done a terrific job, Stevie. I knew you would, too. Nobody but you would have thought to suggest a riding picnic or a mock rodeo. That's the reason I wanted you to volunteer, you know."

"Thanks, Max," she said.

Max cleared his throat. "There's another rider here who seems to think that this kind of project is exactly what she ought to be in charge of."

Stevie knew who he was talking about. "Actually, she just offered to help me in any way she could, but I think that means only if they're rich enough or good-looking enough." Then Stevie blushed. She didn't mean to make catty remarks about Veronica to Max. And she felt strange talking about how good-looking boys were or weren't with him. It was almost like talking about it with her father.

Max chuckled. "Well, I couldn't get any financial

statements, but if you want to know how good-looking the boys are, The Equestrian Exchange—that's the organization that's sponsoring this visit—sent me some pictures of them. I have them here—" He shuffled through the papers on his desk. "—somewhere." He shuffled some more. "Oh, here they are." Max looked at the pictures before handing them over to Stevie. "On second thought, I think you'd better *not* show these to that other rider we were talking about. I suspect she might suddenly try to become your best friend."

Stevie took the pictures from him. Max was right. These guys were definitely good-looking.

"Of course, the pictures might be touched up. The boys might not be as good-looking in real life," Max teased.

With a straight face, Stevie told him, "The looks of a rider don't matter. It's skill that counts!"

"You're right, Stevie," Max said seriously. "But, of course, that's only when he's on the horse. Now, when a rider is off his horse, the 'looks' issue becomes a little more important, doesn't it?"

"Maybe to somebody like Veronica diAngelo, but as far as I'm concerned, I'll be pleased to escort these guys anywhere, anytime, on horseback, or otherwise."

Max laughed. "Good. Now, here's their schedule. I'll be picking them up at the airport on the Thursday. You can come with me. I'll take the eight-passenger van."

Max had quite a bit more to say, but Stevie found her mind wandering a bit. She folded the schedule and put it in her pocket along with her list of activities. She couldn't wait to get back to Carole and Lisa to let them know how cute the boys were—and how jealous Veronica was going to be!

At last Max finished talking.

"Okay, thanks, Max. I'll see you tomorrow," she said on her way out of his office.

Carole and Lisa were grooming Starlight when Stevie joined them. Automatically, she picked up a brush and joined in. One of the good things about horses was that they were big enough so that three best friends could groom one of them together. Starlight seemed to love the attention.

"Max just gave me the schedule for the Italian boys," Stevie announced. "I saw their pictures. Veronica is going to scream when she sees them. She's going to be so jealous!"

She filled her friends in on what Max had said and told them about some of the fun things she had in mind for them. She left out the tobogganing and water slide ideas.

"A picnic! I love it!" Carole exclaimed. "Oh, it's going to be a wonderful four days!"

"It definitely is," Stevie agreed. "Especially since a certain Veronica diAngelo is going to be furious and jealous every single minute of those four days!"

"Imagine Veronica being jealous of you—and us," Lisa added. "It's going to be great."

"I'm not so sure," Carole said. "Veronica isn't the type to be jealous and not do anything about it. The girl will act, believe me. I don't know what she'll do, but it'll be something, and it'll be something bad."

Stevie shook her head. "I don't think so. Look, if she tries anything, she'll just get in hot water with Max. I don't think she wants to do that, do you?"

"I don't think Max is going to be her target. I think Stevie is her target," Carole said ominously.

"Oh, phooey," Stevie said. "Who cares about dumb old Veronica?"

The question hung in the air.

Mrs. Reg, Max's mother, came over to Starlight's stall. "Oh, there you are, Stevie," she said. "You just got a phone call. It was your brother, Alex. Something about a bicycle? It wasn't too clear, but he said that if he didn't get it back right away, some picture of somebody named Phil was going to disappear."

"He *wouldn't!*" Stevie cried.

"I don't know about that," Mrs. Reg said. "But he didn't seem awfully happy."

"Talk to you later!" Stevie said. She tossed Starlight's brush into his grooming bucket and ran for Alex's bike. She got on and began pumping as hard as she could to get home as fast as possible. She couldn't let Alex rip up her picture of Phil! Brothers were just awful. Why did she have to have three of them?

It didn't really occur to Stevie that this situation was partly her fault, and that she'd been asking for trouble when she took her brother's bike without asking.

If he lays one dirty mitt on that picture, she thought grimly, *I'll—I'll tell every girl in his class what a gross person he really is . . . and . . .*

It also didn't occur to Stevie that the thoughts that were running through her head weren't exactly appropriate for a person who had recently discovered the joys of doing things for others. Her thoughts were decidedly uncharitable.

Stevie pedaled as fast and as hard as she could. She knew it was a good thing that the roads were empty because she wasn't being careful at all. She wasn't paying anywhere near enough attention to things as they whizzed past her. The only thing she noticed, in fact, was a poster with a girl on it that somebody had put up on a lamppost near Fenton Hall.

Alex was standing on the Lakes's front lawn when Stevie arrived.

"About time!" he said. "You had no right—"

"You didn't hurt the picture, did you?" Stevie interrupted.

"No, but next time I will."

"Sorry," she said, handing him the bike.

"Stevie, phone for you!" her older brother Chad called out the upstairs window. "Some guy named Phil. That's the one you're trying to dump, isn't it? Should I tell him you're on a date or something?"

Since Chad was yelling loud enough for all of downtown Willow Creek to hear what he was saying, Stevie figured that Phil had probably heard him, too. One of the nice things about Phil was that he understood when things like this happened, because he had as many sisters as she had brothers.

Stevie was glad now that she'd rushed home. Otherwise, she might have missed Phil's call. She wanted to tell him about everything that was going to happen. She reached for the phone and paused. On second thought, she decided, she didn't have to tell him everything. Phil probably didn't need to know how good-looking the Italian boys were.

5

STEVIE GOT AN early start for school the next morning. *After all*, she told herself, *a person who is turning over a new leaf shouldn't be following a lot of bad habits.* She also knew that she wouldn't get away with being late two mornings in a row!

It was a lovely spring morning. The forsythia was in bloom and the fruit trees in people's yards were beginning to bud. The air was clean and fresh. A cool breeze brushed through Stevie's hair. She took a deep breath and gazed up at the clear blue sky. It was a wonderful morning to be alive. Even the fact that she was going to school couldn't ruin it.

Stevie sighed happily. The sky was beautiful. The pale green leaves beginning to appear on the trees were beautiful. The busy birds, flitting from branch to branch, were beautiful. The roofs of the houses, the windows, the porches, were beautiful. *Everything is beautiful,* she thought, *even the telephone pole with the*—Stevie stopped abruptly.

There it was again, the poster with the girl on it. There was something very familiar about the girl, too. Stevie squinted and walked over to it. The first thing that became clear to her were the words: FOR PRESIDENT. The next thing that became very clear was that somebody had made a bad mistake. There, in front of her, in black and white, was a picture of her. The poster proclaimed that she, Stevie Lake, was running for president of Fenton Hall Middle School.

"No way," she told her likeness on the telephone pole. The picture didn't answer.

Stevie felt a sudden chill, and it wasn't from the morning air. Something very peculiar was going on. She'd decided to turn over a new leaf, not an entire tree! She took a deep breath and read the entire poster from beginning to end.

FOR PRESIDENT
[then came her picture]
STEVIE LAKE
of
Fenton Hall Middle School

A Young Girl with a Big Heart!
Voluntary Chairman of Children's Hospital Festival
Elected Chairman of Fenton Hall Spring Fair
Go with the Best
A Vote for Stevie Is a Vote for Students!
Debates: Saturday the 28th
Election: Monday the 30th

Stevie could hardly believe what she was reading. The office of the President of the Middle School usually went to somebody with really terrific grades who spent a lot of time in the principal's office talking about school projects. Stevie didn't have terrific grades and, although she spent a lot of time in the principal's office, most of it had to do with things she had to promise never to do again!

The President of the Middle School was a person who dedicated his or her time to good projects. The President was the kind of person who cared when somebody whispered in assembly. The President was the kind of person who was always ready to help somebody else, whether it was collecting canned goods for the homeless or giving a student advice on how to get along with a teacher or arranging with the phys. ed. department to have basketballs available for games after lunch.

Stevie, on the other hand, was the kind of person who would bring in cans of food for the homeless—two weeks after the drive was over. She could never tell anybody how to get along with a teacher, but she could tell them how to spread a thin layer of rubber cement under the teacher's desk so the teacher's shoes would stick in it. She never wanted to play basketball after lunch, but she had figured out how to rig the electronic scoreboard so that no matter who scored, the number always showed up in the "Fouls" column.

The person who was President of the Middle School was a person so unlike Stevie Lake that Stevie didn't even know who the last one was!

Suddenly, Stevie was filled with determination. She had to get to the bottom of this. She adjusted her book bag on her shoulder and practically marched the rest of the way to school. She hardly saw the boys and girls who greeted her as she neared the building. She barely heard their congratulations or felt their pats of encouragement. She was rapidly getting used to people clapping her on the back. She made a beeline for Miss Fenton's office and stopped at Miss Ward's desk.

"I'm not running for Middle School President," Stevie said.

The gray-haired lady peered at Stevie over her pale pink glasses. "Oh yes, you are," she said. "I saw the posters. They're all over the place."

"I know they are, but I'm not running," Stevie said patiently.

Miss Ward chuckled. "You're right about that. You'll win walking. Only one other person is running and that's Robert Effingwell. Nobody knows him."

Stevie had the funny feeling she and Miss Ward were talking at cross-purposes. "I mean, I didn't get a lot of signatures on any petitions," she tried to explain.

"You got enough," Miss Ward said.

"I did?"

"Let me see," Miss Ward said. She disappeared suddenly under the counter, crouching to pull something from a file. A moment later, her head popped up. "Here it is," she said, producing some crumpled papers. "The student government rules state that you must have twenty-five signatures to place your name in nomination. You have over a hundred. There's no problem at all. You're running all right."

"I am?"

"You are." Miss Ward handed the petition to Stevie as if it proved something. Stevie gazed at the papers in front of her. Miss Ward was right. There were more than a hundred signatures on them. Somehow, she was running for President of the Middle School.

"Thanks," Stevie managed to say.

"You're welcome," Miss Ward told her. Then the first bell rang. All the extra time Stevie had given herself by leaving home early had disappeared when she'd discovered she was running for office. Now, she had to dash just to get to her homeroom on time.

She turned and began running. Then she stopped herself. A girl who expected people to vote for her wouldn't ever do anything as undignified as racing along the hallway. She decided to walk fast instead.

PEPPER WAS ACTING up a little as Lisa tried to saddle him that afternoon before riding class. Every time she tried to pull the buckle on his girth one hole tighter, he'd take a deep breath, expanding his belly so much that she couldn't tighten it.

"What do I do, Stevie?" Lisa called over the stall divider to where Stevie was finishing tacking up her horse, Topside.

"Put on the bridle and then try again," Stevie replied. "Try to catch him off guard. If that doesn't work, you'll just have to adjust it when you're in the saddle."

Lisa reached for the bridle and began to put it on Pepper. She straightened out all the leathers and then slipped the bit into his mouth.

"I'm running for Middle School President," Stevie called casually over the divider.

"What?" Lisa let the bit drop back out of Pepper's mouth because she was laughing so hard. "Funny thing," she said between giggles. "I thought I just heard you say you were running for Middle School President."

"I did," Stevie told her.

"What?" Lisa asked.

"I said, and I quote, 'I'm running for Middle School President.'"

"*You?*"

"Is somebody else here?" Stevie asked.

"I'm here, what's up?" Carole said breezily, walking Starlight along the hallway between the stalls where Lisa and Stevie were tacking up.

"Stevie's running for Middle School President," Lisa told Carole.

"At Fenton Hall?" Carole asked, stunned. She knew she'd heard Lisa right. She just didn't believe it.

"That's the Middle School I go to," Stevie said. A little bit of irritation had crept into her voice.

Carole grinned. "Fenton Hall will never be the same."

"Hey, guys, give me a break, will you?" Stevie asked. "Maybe I'm the one who's going to change. After all, I'm the one who's going to be escorting the Italian riders around and I'm the one who's in charge of the Children's Hospital Festival." Stevie made a final adjustment on Topside's girth and then slid open his stall door. She led him into the hall, next to where Carole stood. "And look at this," Stevie said. She reached into her back pocket and pulled out one of her campaign posters. Dozens of them had been taped up in the school hallways. She didn't think one less would make much difference. "I took it down for my scrapbook," she explained rather sheepishly. "Anyway, look at this. I've got lots of qualifications for the presidency."

"Sure. Biggest troublemaker in the school," Lisa suggested. "Where does it say that?"

Stevie looked annoyed. "It doesn't say that. It says that I'm the Voluntary Chairman of the Children's Hospital Festival. Now that's a person who cares about others and who cares about her school. That's a person who can really give her all to representing her schoolmates' best interests. Even if it's my first elected office—"

"Spare me the speech," Carole interrupted, "and tell me what this Spring Fair is that you got elected to."

"Spring Fair? I don't know. I've never heard of it. What's a Spring Fair?" Stevie asked.

"Sounds like some sort of fund-raiser for the school," Lisa suggested. "When was it?"

"*Was?* Spring has just started. Anything called a Spring Fair ought to be coming up soon," Carole said.

"Must be some kind of mistake," Stevie said, dismissing her friends' concern. "Maybe it was something I did last year that I've just forgotten about. What interests me now are the things I'm *going* to be doing. You see, I seem to be a person other people like to count on to help them. Like you, for instance, Lisa. Let's check on Pepper's girth now, okay?"

Lisa and Carole were used to Stevie's willingness to

help them whenever they needed it. They weren't used to her being so expansive about it.

"Everything she's said since she got here sounds like a campaign speech," Lisa said to Carole.

"And we can't even vote for her," Carole added.

"I'm just trying to turn over a new leaf," Stevie said defensively, a little surprised by her friends' response.

"We like the old leaf just fine," Lisa said.

"Come on. Let's get to class," Carole reminded them. She had the feeling that this conversation wasn't getting them anywhere but into trouble.

The three girls led their horses to the outdoor ring, brushed the stable's traditional good luck horseshoe, and mounted. Veronica and Garnet were right behind them.

"Say, Veronica," Lisa said. "When's the Fenton Hall Spring Fair?"

"Um, let me think," Veronica said, making a show of putting her index finger to her chin. "The Spring Fair, hmmmmm. Oh, yes, that's always the last Saturday of this month. Are you planning to come?" Lisa thought she saw a slight smirk cross Veronica's face, but there was nothing new about that. Slight smirks were always crossing Veronica's face.

"I wouldn't miss it for the world," Lisa replied.

"Me neither," Veronica said. This time her smirk was unmistakable, and something about it made Lisa very nervous.

6

"So TELL US about your bright idea for the Children's Hospital Festival," Lisa said to Stevie on Friday night. "You said it had something to do with horses, didn't you?"

The three girls were having a sleep-over party at Carole's house, and for them, sleep-overs always turned into long Saddle Club meetings. Carole was lying face down on her bed, with her chin resting on her hands. Lisa was sitting on an upholstered chair by the closet door, and Stevie was sitting cross-legged on the floor. Carole's coal-black cat, Snowball—so named because she always did the exact opposite of what anybody told her to do—was curled up and sleeping soundly on Stevie's lap. Stevie continued to pat the cat gently as she spoke.

"Okay, but I haven't gotten very far. What I want to do is have some kind of riding demonstration. Then I want to get Max to let us use his pony cart to give the kids rides. Maybe we could even saddle one of the ponies and give rides to anyone who could sit up in one. What do you think?"

"Put the patients on horses?" Carole asked.

Stevie nodded. "Think it's a bad idea?"

"No. I think it's a fabulous idea," Carole told her. She thought about the sad and bad times in her life. No matter what was going on, she'd always had riding to comfort her. "It's a great activity to share with other kids, even— or maybe especially—if they've got troubles."

"Will Max go along with it?" Lisa asked.

"I don't know," Stevie said. "I know he's pretty happy with the stuff I'm doing for him with the Italian boys— not that that's any trouble. So he really ought to be nice about this."

"Sure, and you could always get Miss Fenton to call him, if necessary," Carole suggested. She smiled. She'd never met Miss Fenton, but she'd heard a lot about her from Stevie. The image of laid-back Max and uptight Miss Fenton talking was very funny.

"What a pair they would make," Stevie mused, obviously thinking along the same lines as Carole. "On second thought, I think I'll take care of it myself."

"You're taking care of a lot of stuff yourself," Lisa reminded her. "Speaking of which, what happened with the Spring Fair?"

Stevie shrugged. "I'm helpless on that one. I guess I *did* run for chairman, though I thought I was sick the day they had the nominations. Anyway, that's something we pretty much do the same way every year. Everything is stored away. I just have to get people to set up the booths. And, of course, I've got to find people to do stuff like bake cookies."

"That reminds me," Lisa interrupted. "Didn't I see some brownie mix in your kitchen when we were eating supper? It looked like it was just sitting on the counter, dying for somebody to come along and crack an egg, add water and oil, maybe some walnuts, and chocolate chips. What do you think?" she asked Carole.

"Okay," Carole agreed, "but you know what my father's like when we bake something."

They did know what Carole's father was like. He was one of their favorite people. Sometimes Carole teased Stevie that she was only her friend so she could spend time with Colonel Hanson.

"Yeah, we know," Lisa said, pretending that it was a grave problem.

"He's going to want to lick the bowl," Carole warned.

Stevie grinned. "That's fine, as long as I get dibs on the spoon! Come on, Snowball, stay asleep," she commanded. Snowball woke up immediately and bounded out of Stevie's lap.

The three girls headed for the kitchen. As Carole had predicted, Colonel Hanson, who had been watching television, soon joined them there.

"I love it when you three beautiful ladies get together," he said.

"Don't worry, Dad," Carole told him. "You can lay off the flattery. We've already decided you can lick the bowl."

"I've raised a mind reader!" He laughed.

"Now there's an idea," Stevie said, putting a bowl on the counter.

"For what?" the colonel asked.

"For my school fair," Stevie said. "See, I'm chairman of it, and we've got all these booths and stuff, but I get to decide if there are going to be any new things to do. I like the idea of having a mind reader. We could get a crystal ball or something and set up a mind reader, fortune-teller type thing. Like it?"

"I *love* it," Lisa said, cracking an egg. "And even if nobody goes to it, you can still make a fortune. Get it? A *fortune?*"

Stevie and Carole groaned. Colonel Hanson chuckled. "That's so bad it's funny." He loved corny old jokes and often swapped especially awful ones with Stevie.

Carole measured the water and oil, added them to the mix in the bowl, and handed Stevie a wooden spoon. Stevie began stirring carefully. "Carole, why don't you chop the walnuts. And Lisa, see if you can find some chocolate chips. Then grease the bottom of the baking dish."

"Aye aye, ma'am," Carole said. She and Lisa saluted and then followed instructions.

Colonel Hanson raised his eyebrows. "She's gotten a promotion to boss these days?" he asked Carole and Lisa.

Carole looked up from the pile of walnuts she was about to chop. "Of the whole wide world," she said.

"It's a new leaf," Lisa explained solemnly.

"Come on, guys. Give me a break, will you?" Stevie asked.

"Sure, but why don't you tell Dad all the things you're doing these days?" Carole said. "You're going to be so busy we'll never even see you at Pine Hollow any more."

The fact was that Carole was worried about everything Stevie had taken on. It wasn't that Stevie wasn't capable of doing these things. She was. She could do every one of them and more. The problem was that they were all coming up soon. Even though some of them, such as the Italian boys project and the Hospital Festival, would be vaguely related to horses, they were all going to cut seriously into Stevie's riding time.

Carole continued to voice her concern. "I mean, are

you even going to have time to come to Pony Club meetings?"

"Of course I am," Stevie said positively. "I wouldn't miss my riding for anything, any more than I would miss spending time with you two—uh, three," she corrected herself, glancing at Carole's father.

"Thanks," he said, pleased to be included. "But tell me what you're doing that's got my daughter so upset."

"She shouldn't be upset," Stevie began. "She should be excited for me. After all—"

The phone rang. Since all three girls were involved in the brownie-making, Colonel Hanson answered it. As soon as they heard him say "Oh, hi, Frank," they were interested.

Frank was Frank Devine, a retired Marine Corps friend of Colonel Hanson. He was also the father of Katharine Devine, better known as Kate, one of the Saddle Club's out-of-town members. Kate had been a championship rider in the horse show circuit, but had given it up when she found that the competition had interfered with her enjoyment of riding. She'd only started riding again when the Saddle Club had roped her into helping them with a gymkhana. Now her family ran a dude ranch in the Southwest, and she'd taken up another kind of riding. Stevie, Lisa, and Carole had visited her twice. They couldn't wait for another chance to see her. All three of them wondered the same thing as they listened to Carole's father on the phone. Was this the chance?

"Spring break, huh? Christine, too?"

Carole's eyes widened. This was sounding good. Christine Lonetree was also an out-of-town Saddle Club member. She was a Native American girl who lived a few miles from Kate. The girls had met her on their visits to the Bar-None Ranch.

"No, Carole's in school then," Colonel Hanson was saying. "Her spring break isn't until—"

The girls looked at each other. Now, it wasn't sounding so good.

"Oh, I suppose it would be fun for them—"

All pretense of brownie-making had stopped.

"But there's no way—"

What was going on?

Colonel Hanson laughed into the phone. "No, I mean there's no way I could say no. Carole would never speak to me again—to say nothing of Stevie and Lisa—"

That sounded much better!

"Okay, so that's the fourth weekend of the month. Let's see . . . wait a minute. I just need to find—" Colonel Hanson looked around. The girls sprang to his assistance. Carole handed him a calendar, Lisa gave him a pencil, and Stevie offered a scrap of paper. He accepted the things with a wink.

He looked at the calendar, scribbled something down

on the paper, and spoke. "All right, we'll see all three of you then."

"We will?" all three girls asked at once. The colonel nodded and listened.

"Okay, I'll wait to hear from you then, and somebody will meet the girls. It's too bad you have to go right back," he said.

It can only mean one thing, Carole hoped. She held her breath while her father finished his conversation.

"All right. Good-bye. Love to Phyllis," he told Frank, then hung up.

"So?" Carole asked, about to explode with excitement.

"You think that had something to do with you?" he teased.

"Come on, Dad," Carole pleaded. "We can't stand the suspense."

Colonel Hanson smiled and hugged his daughter. "Well, my dears," he told all three girls, "it turns out that Frank's piloting skills are needed." Frank, a former Marine Corps pilot, sometimes flew a plane for a wealthy neighbor with business in Washington. "He'll be making a couple of round trips at times that coincide with Kate and Christine's spring break. Now, it's not your spring break, but I thought you all could enjoy a visit anyway. So, they're coming the fourth weekend of the month and staying for a week."

Carole whooped. "It's going to be fabulous! Imagine, both Kate and Christine here for a visit at the same time. Isn't it wonderful?"

Lisa hugged her friend with excitement. "And they'll be here in less than three weeks!" she shouted gleefully. "Won't it be wonderful, Stevie?"

Stevie nodded, but something about Lisa's words bothered her. Suddenly she didn't feel very good. She put down her wooden spoon and picked up the calendar.

Colonel Hanson had circled the date of Kate and Christine's arrival. They were coming on the fourth weekend of the month. Stevie counted off the days carefully. She looked again and counted again. Lisa was right: It was less than three weeks away.

"Isn't it exciting, Stevie?" Lisa asked again. "Stevie?"

Stevie just stared at the calendar.

"Too much excitement for you, Stevie?" Carole teased.

"Yes," Stevie said glumly.

Her friends fell silent. As long as they'd known Stevie, there had never been such a thing as too much excitement for her.

"What's she staring at?" Lisa asked at last.

"The calendar," Colonel Hanson said.

"Is there a problem with it?" Carole asked.

Stevie nodded numbly.

"What is it?" Carole wanted to know.

"The fourth weekend of the month," Stevie said mechanically. "It's less than three weeks away."

Carole nodded. "Right, so—"

"The Italian boys arrive in three weeks," Stevie said.

"Oh," Lisa said. "Well, it's really not a problem. After all, they'll probably be thrilled to meet the famous Katharine Devine. Or are you worried that they'll think she's better than they are?"

Stevie didn't answer the question. She kept counting the days on the calendar. It all came up the same. She tried to explain, but she was so upset she knew she wasn't doing a good job of it.

"The end of the month is also in three weeks," Stevie managed to say.

"Right," Lisa agreed. "Thirty days hath September and all that. The fourth weekend *is* the end of the—oh, no."

Stevie knew that Lisa had just understood the seriousness of the situation.

"What's going on here?" Carole demanded.

"The end of the month is when the Hospital Festival is taking place," Lisa explained.

Carole's eyes widened. "Oh, no."

"And that's not all," Stevie said. She'd finally gotten her voice back.

Carole, Lisa, and Colonel Hanson waited.

"The end of the month includes the last Saturday of the month," Stevie said.

Lisa and Carole looked at each other. Colonel Hanson just looked puzzled.

"That's when the Spring Fair is supposed to take place," Lisa explained.

"And that's not all," Stevie said dolefully. Her fingers traced the path of the short weeks between the date she was thinking of and the end of the month. It always came up the same.

"The end of the month includes the weekend of the 28th."

"So what momentous event happens on the 28th?" Colonel Hanson asked.

"Debates for President of the Middle School," Stevie informed him.

"Goodness!" he exclaimed. "My dear, if you can handle all of these things at once, you don't need to worry about becoming President of the Middle School. You'll be qualified to be president of the United States!"

"*If* I can get it all done," Stevie said ominously, and her friends agreed.

7

Lisa and Carole walked slowly together toward Pine Hollow after school on Tuesday. Normally the excitement of an upcoming riding class made the two of them chatter nonstop on their way. But today neither of them was in a very talkative mood. Ever since Saturday, Lisa had been consumed with worry for Stevie. She suspected Carole felt the same way.

"She's just got to give up some of it," Lisa said out loud.

"That's just what I was thinking," Carole agreed.

Carole had understood right away what Lisa meant. The same thing was on both of their minds: Stevie was in trouble.

"I don't know how—" Lisa began.

"She can't," Carole said simply.

"You're right."

They walked on in silence.

Ever since Saturday, Lisa had been upset. After Stevie had discovered that everything in the world was going to happen on the last weekend of the month, she'd refused to talk about it. She just kept saying that she'd turned over a new leaf and she'd handle it. To Lisa, it seemed as if Stevie wasn't turning over a new leaf at all—or at least not a good new leaf. Stevie's old leaf had constantly been in hot water. Her new one was heading for boiling point!

Even if it was possible that Stevie might somehow pull everything off and manage to host the Italians, entertain the young hospital patients, run for Middle School President, preside over the Spring Fair, *and* visit with Kate and Christine all at exactly the same time, one thing was certain: her grades would suffer.

And the problem with that—aside from Stevie's own parents—was Max. He took riding seriously, but he took school work even more seriously. All his riders were required to maintain a decent average if they wanted to continue to ride at Pine Hollow. The schools in Willow Creek knew it, too. When averages dropped, Max heard about it, and riders were suspended until the averages came back up. It was an ironclad rule.

There was no doubt that Stevie was smart, but she sometimes let her grades slip. Lisa and Carole had often helped her get her grades back on track in the past. But with all the activities Stevie had planned for the next month, Lisa figured there was no way that Stevie could keep her grades up. Carole was worried about Stevie cutting back on her riding to do all the things she had to do. Lisa was worried about Stevie having to cut out her riding altogether. Who knew how long it would take for her grades to recover?

Lisa sighed. "Oh, no."

Carole didn't even ask what was bothering her. She knew.

"HI, STEVIE," VERONICA diAngelo greeted her warmly, peering over the top of Topside's stall, where Stevie was preparing the horse for class.

Stevie looked at her suspiciously. Something was up. Veronica diAngelo was never, ever warm, especially to her.

Stevie grunted in response.

"All your plans coming along smoothly?" Veronica asked.

Stevie grunted again.

"I know you're going to be a wonderful Fair chairman," Veronica continued. "That's why I nominated you. We really needed somebody we could count on." With those words, Veronica ducked back into her own stall.

Stevie didn't grunt that time. She was too surprised. *Veronica* had nominated her? The thought had never crossed her mind. She didn't think that Veronica would have been willing to say that she could do anything, much less run a whole fair by herself. What had made Veronica do it?

Stevie slid Topside's bridle on and slipped the bit into his mouth.

"What does she want?" Stevie quietly asked the horse.

Topside didn't answer.

"I mean, Veronica never does anything without a reason," Stevie elaborated. She buckled the bridle and laid the reins flat on Topside's neck. "As far as I know, the only thing I've got that Veronica wants is four Italian boys and there's no way—"

Then Stevie started to get a very bad feeling. It began in her toes as a mild tingling and quickly spread upwards to her stomach, which churned with a sickening lurch.

"Oh, no," she told Topside, who seemed unaffected by her tone of voice.

She hoisted his saddle and the saddle pad, placed it so it overlapped his withers, and slid it back until it was properly positioned.

"I smell a rat and her name is Veronica," Stevie muttered.

She reached under the horse, grasped the girth that dangled on the ground from the other side of the saddle, and brought it up to Topside's left side for buckling. She yanked it tight and pushed the metal prongs through the buckle holes. Then she tugged, tightening the girth and making the saddle snug and safe.

Topside regarded her carefully. He wasn't used to having her pull the girth so tight so quickly.

"Sorry, fella," she said, patting his neck in apology. "See, I just got to thinking about something—"

"You need some help?" Carole asked, peering at her friend. Stevie was obviously almost finished tacking up Topside, but class was about to start.

"You bet I do," Stevie said, giving the girth a final tug. "And I'll tell you about it later!"

Carole was puzzled, but there was no time to ask Stevie what she meant. The P.A. announced that class was about to begin.

Stevie slid Topside's door open. "Ready?"

Before Carole could answer, Stevie had headed for the indoor ring. There was a determination in her friend's step that Carole recognized as a sign that something serious was going on. Because of Max's strict rules about talking in class, there was no way she'd learn what it was until class was over. Carole entered the ring herself just in time to hear Max say, "Riders up!"

FROM THE LOOK on Stevie's face, Lisa knew that something was on her friend's mind, and it wasn't going to be anything about new leaves. The excited look of the old, mischievous Stevie was there in full force.

"So what is it?" Lisa asked.

"Come sit down," Stevie invited her, patting the bench next to her in the tack room. Stevie had managed to whisper a message about a Saddle Club meeting in the tack room after class. Now it was about to start. "We have a lot to talk about," Stevie said. "Everybody take a piece of tack and some saddle soap."

At Pine Hollow, the riders were allowed to hang around as much as they wanted, as long as they were doing something useful. Cleaning tack qualified as something useful. It also meant they could be together and talk while they were working.

"I've figured it out," Stevie began.

Lisa saw the twinkle in her friend's eyes. She could hardly wait to hear what was coming.

"The mess I'm in is all Veronica's fault," Stevie continued. "See, I didn't actually volunteer to head the Hospital Festival."

"You didn't?" Carole asked. Stevie shook her head. "Then how did you get to be in charge?" Carole wanted to know.

"Veronica volunteered me," Stevie said simply. "And I didn't circulate a petition to run for President of the Middle School."

"Do we have to ask who did?" Carole said.

"Veronica," Lisa supplied.

"And I definitely did not enter my name in the election for chairman of the Spring Fair," Stevie said.

"Veronica again?" Lisa asked.

"Go to the head of the class," Stevie told her.

"But it doesn't make sense," Carole protested. "Why would Veronica try to make you into some kind of hero?"

"She isn't," Stevie explained. "She's trying to make me go so crazy that I won't be able to do everything at once."

"Well, you can't," Lisa said sensibly. "You're going to have to give up some of it."

"And play right into her slimy little hands?" Stevie asked.

"What are you talking about?" Carole asked.

Stevie scooped a generous glob of saddle soap out of the container and began rubbing it vigorously onto Topside's saddle. "It all has to do with the Italian boys," she said. "Veronica is trying to force me to give up the job of hosting them. She wants them all to herself!"

"You've got too much there," Carole said, taking some of Stevie's soap. She worked it into the bridle she was cleaning.

"I'll take some, too," Lisa said. Stevie offered her a third of the soap.

"That's what friends are for," Stevie said. "I knew I could count on you."

Lisa looked up from the bridle she was cleaning. "I'm getting a funny feeling about this," she said to Carole.

Carole nodded.

Before Carole or Lisa could ask Stevie exactly what she'd meant by that remark, Mrs. Reg appeared. As well as being Max's mother, the riders thought she was a kind of part-time mother to all of the riders as well. That included the bossy side of mothering as well as the loving support.

"I trust you aren't talking so much that no work is getting done," she said.

"No, Mrs. Reg," Stevie said. "Believe me, a *lot* of work is getting done."

She said it so positively that everybody looked at her a little oddly.

"Hmmm. All this chatter reminds me of something," Mrs. Reg said. Everyone looked up eagerly. Mrs. Reg was famous for telling the most astonishing stories about horses and riders. But nobody had ever found a way of talking her either into or out of telling one of her stories. When she had something to say, she said it.

"What's that, Mrs. Reg?" Carole asked.

"Reminds me of a rider we had here a long time ago. Important man, he was," she began. She sat down on one of the benches near Stevie and picked up a sponge and a bridle. She talked best when she was soaping leathers. "Mr. Dunellen, I think that was his name. He appeared here one day and told my husband, Max—your Max's father—that he'd just bought two horses, and he wanted to ride them every day. At first, Max was pretty happy about that. Times were thin then, and a paying boarder was very welcome. Then the man brought them in. One was a bay mare, the other a gelding, gray, I think. Anyway, he told Max he was going to ride every day."

"Lucky guy," Carole remarked. "He must have been a millionaire, huh?"

"No, he was just the town pharmacist," Mrs. Reg replied. "Didn't make a lot of money at that, though he paid his bill on time every month. Well, Max predicted that this man was going to be more trouble than he was worth. Said the man had too much to do to ride every day. Said he'd be calling in all the time and getting us to exercise those horses."

"Why was that?" Stevie asked.

Mrs. Reg appeared to ignore the interruption. One of the things about her stories was that she told them exactly the way she wanted to tell them.

"That Mr. Dunellen was one of the busiest men in town," Mrs. Reg went on. "See, because he was the only pharmacist in town at that time, he always knew who was sick and who wasn't. He always took the time to do something nice when people were laid up—you know, call on them with a bunch of flowers, a covered dish. Whatever he thought they needed, he'd just do it. Then, a lot of people sort of thought he was a doctor and they'd come to him when they were sick. Often, he'd end up delivering medicine to them, even did it himself when his delivery boy was off. He sang in the church choir. He was a tenor, and never missed a Sunday. People trusted him. Eventually, because everybody knew him, he ended up being elected mayor. If somebody had a problem, Mayor Dunellen would go there and solve it on the spot."

"Boy, I bet you and Max ended up exercising his horses for him all the time, didn't you?" Lisa asked.

Mrs. Reg looked at her with a puzzled expression on her face. "Oh, no, not at all," Mrs. Reg said. Then, without any further explanation, she stood up, hung up the now clean bridle, and returned to her office. One of the other things about Mrs. Reg's stories was that she often ended them just when they were beginning to get very interesting. Lisa thought it was a bad habit.

For a moment no one spoke. Then Lisa turned to her friends. "So what was that all about?"

"Beats me." Carole shrugged. "I mean, it sounds like the man had this incredible schedule and there was no way he could take the time to ride."

"You two!" Stevie said, beaming. "Don't you get it?"

"Get what?" Lisa asked. She was a little annoyed. She didn't like it when somebody else understood something that was a mystery to her.

"How he rode, of course," Stevie said.

"I guess he hired somebody else to exercise the horses," Carole suggested.

Stevie grimaced. "No, he didn't. Didn't you hear what Mrs. Reg just said? That's not what that story is about. He rode all the time. He used his horses to make his visits to sick people, to deliver medicines, and to be on the spot when he was mayor. He probably even used the horses to ride to church on Sundays when he had to sing in the choir."

"Oh," Carole said. "I get it now."

"I guess he was pretty smart," Lisa said. "He figured out a way to combine two things he wanted to do so they only took up the time of one."

"You know, it's a little bit like my mother once said to me," Carole said. "She told me that if something was important to me, I'd find a way to do it."

"My thought exactly!" Stevie said, a gleam in her eye.

"I know that look," Lisa said, recognizing it from the many times when Stevie had come up with some kind of impossible scheme—and had pulled it off successfully!

"So, what's the most important thing you've got to do?" Carole asked.

"Beat Veronica," Stevie said. "And I know just how we're going to do it!"

"We?" Carole asked dubiously.

"I'm in," Lisa said.

Carole sighed. "Me too," she said.

STEVIE LEANED BACK in Max's eight-passenger van and sighed. It felt like the first time she had relaxed in almost three weeks. As she thought about the days that had just flown by, she was sure that was the case.

Since her terrible discovery of Veronica's plot, Stevie and her friends had been working at nonstop, breakneck speed. So far, everything was looking good.

A lot of Stevie's work had been done on the telephone. She'd had to talk to the hospital administrators, who were thrilled with her ideas. She'd also had to talk to Miss Fenton, who was less enthusiastic, and to Max, who was downright dubious. Finally, she'd had to talk to her opponent in the presidential race. He had given her his total cooperation. There were a few people she hadn't talked to. For instance, she hadn't talked to Kate and Christine and told them what parts she wanted them to play in her plans. And she hadn't talked to the Italian boys. She wasn't even sure if she would be able to talk to them, if they didn't know any English.

The people she'd been talking to most of all had been Lisa and Carole. That first afternoon, in the tack room, she'd talked a lot and she hadn't thought it was going to do any good.

"Don't you see what Mrs. Reg is telling us?" she had asked.

"Us?" Carole had said.

"Yeah, *us*. The answer is in making everything happen at the same time," she had said.

"It *is* happening at the same time," Lisa had reminded her. "That's the problem!"

"Right," she had replied. "So, now what we have to do is to make it all happen at the same place."

Seventy-three phone calls later, it had all been settled. The hospital had agreed to let the school use its grounds for the school's Spring Fair, which was where the Hospital Festival would also take place, and where the candidates' speeches would be delivered. All of this was going to happen with the help of the Saddle Club, including all of its out-of-town members and, with some luck, the Italian equestrian team.

Stevie sat up. "Uh, Max," she began tentatively. "I have a little favor to ask you."

He glanced at her quickly. "Well, Stevie, you can try, but right now I'm having a little touble keeping track of all the favors I'm already doing you."

Stevie really hoped he was joking.

"It's about Saturday," she began. "See, the boys' first demonstration is scheduled for late afternoon, but I've got something else right then that I have to do. Can Carole and Lisa be their hostess for that?" She wasn't sure exactly how truthful to be. After all, if Max found out how many things she had going at once, he might decide that she shouldn't take on the extra responsibility of the Italian boys. Veronica had taken the time to remind him every day that she'd be more than happy to pitch in.

"Does this have anything to do with Favor Number Two—my pony cart?" Max asked.

"Uh, yes," Stevie said.

Max gripped the wheel of the car tightly. "Stevie, if there is one thing I've learned about you over the years it's that I can't possibly trust you—"

The words hung heavily in the air. Stevie braced herself for the worst.

"—to do anything in the slightest bit predictable," Max finished. "But since I know you've worked so hard to plan a visit for these boys, I don't suppose it will matter if you're not there for an hour or two." Stevie sighed with relief. "Now, about Favor Number—what is it, Three? Where exactly do we have to go first?"

"The private aviation hangar," Stevie replied. "It's on the far side of the airport."

One of the things Stevie had arranged was for Frank Devine's plane to arrive half an hour before the Italian boys. And since they were all going to the same place, Max and Stevie were picking up Kate and Christine as well. "After all," she had reminded Max when she'd requested Favor Number Three, "Kate is a championship rider, too."

"What's that got to do with anything?" Max had asked.

"Nothing," she'd said. "I just thought, well, think of the honor to your van, to have five championship riders in it, all at—"

"I give up! I give up!" Max had cried. "We'll do it."

STEVIE THOUGHT IT was a good sign that Christine and Kate were already waiting for them when they got to the hangar. Frank explained that there had been favorable head winds, so they'd made good time. Stevie had no idea what head winds were, but she was glad for them anyway.

She hugged Kate, Christine, and Frank, and introduced Christine and Frank to Max. Max already knew Kate from her involvement in the gymkhana.

The girls tossed their bags into the back of the van and hopped in, waving goodbye to Frank.

"This is going to be fantastic," Kate said when the girls were settled in their seats. "Christine and I are exhausted from all the work we've been doing at school. We need a nice relaxing vacation."

"Maybe you'd rather try a forced-labor camp, then," Max said drily.

"What's he talking about?" Christine asked suspiciously.

"Oh, well, we've got a few things going on now around here," Stevie explained vaguely.

"I'm getting a funny feeling about this," Kate told Christine.

"Me, too. But, if I remember correctly, funny feelings around Stevie are pretty common and usually turn out okay—hey, didn't you just miss the airport exit? Where are we going?"

"International Arrivals," Stevie said.

FORTY MINUTES LATER, the three girls and Max were looking over a railing onto the customs area, trying to spot the Italian equestrian team.

"Andre, Enrico, Gian, Marco," Stevie mumbled, scanning the crowd.

"What are you saying?" Christine asked.

"Their names," Stevie told her. "Don't they sound wonderfully romantic—Andre, Enrico, Gian, and Marco?"

"Are these guys tall, dark, and handsome?" Christine asked.

"Yes," Stevie said.

"Are they probably carrying bulky bags with things like riding boots and saddles in them?" Christine wanted to know.

"Yes," Stevie said again.

"Well, then, I think those four handsome guys over there with all the bulky luggage are our guys," Kate said. "Come on!"

Kate led Christine, Stevie, and Max to the lower level where the four boys would emerge as soon as they'd cleared customs. There was a crowd of people at the door and a crowd of people coming through the door. Stevie stood on her toes and strained her eyes, eager for the moment when Andre, Enrico, Gian, and Marco would appear.

And then, there they were. For three weeks, Stevie had been trying to imagine what it would be like to actually meet these boys. She'd been gazing at their pictures and practicing useful Italian phrases. Now, meeting them, she realized that every second of that time had been wasted. Stevie couldn't even mutter a weak *buon giorno,* or hello. Instead, she reached out her hand and said, "*Arrivederci,*" which was Italian for goodbye!

"So soon?" the first boy said, a grin crossing his face.

He shook Stevie's hand. "We haven't even been introduced yet, you know."

Stevie almost gaped. "You speak English?" she asked.

"Sure, I do. So do we all. And from the sound of it, our English is better than your Italian, but maybe not as charming. My name is Marco, by the way."

"I'm Stevie," she said, once again offering him the hand he'd just shaken. This time he kissed it. Stevie blushed.

The next few minutes were a massive confusion of introductions and luggage hauling. Stevie tried to shake everybody's hand and help with all of their luggage, but by the time she'd picked up three suitcases, she couldn't take anybody's hand. She also found herself in the middle of introducing Christine, Kate, and Max, and got so confused trying to remember which was Enrico and which was Andre, to say nothing of Gian and Marco, that she almost forgot Max's name.

Finally, when everybody had grasped all the bags they could carry and all the names they could remember, Max led the way to the van. Stevie eyed the luggage and wondered if four saddles, four boot bags, four suitcases, and four good-looking Italian boys would fit in the van. She decided that somehow they'd find a way!

Stevie had spent a fair amount of time—more than she ever would have confessed to Veronica—worrying about what she was going to say to the Italian boys, how she would treat them, and how they all would get along.

She saw with relief that all of that time had been wasted. The four boys chattered easily with Stevie, Christine, and Kate. They were thrilled to learn that they were actually riding with *the* Kate Devine, former riding champion. And they'd never thought they would actually meet a real Native American.

"But where is your war paint?" Enrico teased.

"Back home with my bows and arrows and my scalp collection. And how have you packed your pizzas?" Christine joked.

Stevie laughed, too, recalling her own misconceptions when she'd first met Christine.

"First stop, Pine Hollow," Max announced. "I'll drop you all off there with your saddles, and I'll take the luggage back to my house. Stevie, you're the tour guide. Take everybody around. Have a good time!"

Stevie, Christine, and Kate helped the boys unload their saddles. Kate and Christine took out their luggage as well. Then they all waved goodbye to Max. The boys laughed when they saw that he was actually only driving about twenty extra feet to get to the driveway of his house.

"*Andiamo!*" Stevie announced brightly, finally remembering a useful Italian phrase. What she'd said was, "Let's go."

"Very good. Your Italian has improved tremendously already!" Marco teased.

Stevie didn't mind being teased. She had a feeling that everything was going to go just fine from here on out.

Stevie led the way through the stable, showing the boys the tack room first so they could put down their saddles. She was proud of Pine Hollow and pleased at the chance to show it off to her new friends. She walked down the main walkway with them and introduced them to some of her favorite horses, including Topside, who had had a distinguished career as a show horse. One of the boys would no doubt be riding him for the demonstration. She also showed them Starlight, Delilah, a pretty palomino, and her colt, Samson. They all admired Samson's mane and his beautiful sleek black coat.

Stevie enjoyed showing Christine and the boys everything on the tour, but her very favorite part was when she got to show them Veronica diAngelo. It seemed that Veronica had found it necessary to groom Garnet that afternoon. Veronica had never done any work at all in her life if she could help it. Stevie knew perfectly well that she was just there to look at the boys and to show off. Veronica was decked out in her newest, most fashionable, and most expensive, riding outfit. Garnet was also groomed and gleaming.

"Oh, Veronica," Stevie said sweetly. "I'm glad you're here. I was so afraid I would miss the opportunity to introduce you to Enrico, Andre, Gian, and Marco."

Veronica tried to look up at the boys as if she hadn't

even known they were coming, but she gave herself away when her jaw dropped. The color rose in her face. Although it appeared to be red, Stevie was certain that underneath it all, it was green. Veronica was so jealous, she could hardly speak. Stevie just loved it!

Stevie waved casually to Veronica. "See you around," she said sweetly. Veronica had still not managed to utter a syllable by the time Stevie and her troop rounded the corner to the indoor ring.

When they'd finished their tour of the stable, including the feed room, tack room, locker area, and schooling rings, Stevie knew it was time to get her plan back into action.

"Next stop?" Enrico asked.

"The hospital," Stevie told them.

Six sets of eyes looked at her with concern, to say nothing of confusion.

"Well, there are a few things I need to tell you about," she began.

9

"HAVE YOU SEEN Stevie?" a girl whom Carole didn't know asked her.

"Not since this morning," Carole said. She tried to keep the sharpness out of her voice, but she was getting a little annoyed. She had arrived at the fairground right after school. Stevie and her schoolmates had gotten the day off from school to help set up the fair, but as far as Carole could see, Stevie was nowhere in sight.

Carole stood in the open yard of the hospital grounds. A school fair was slowly growing before her eyes. All around her, wooden booths were being assembled, bolted together and decorated. An oval path had been laid out to one side for the pony cart rides for the hospital patients.

Lisa approached her. "Have you got a hammer?" she asked.

"I loaned it to somebody—I don't know his name—about half an hour ago," Carole replied. "That's the trouble, you know. We don't know anybody's name here."

"Well, we don't go to this school," Lisa reminded her.

"So why are we working so hard for it?" Carole asked a little grumpily.

Lisa shrugged good-naturedly. "Come on, Carole. You know why—" she broke off suddenly. "Hey, here comes somebody who can personally answer that question for us. Unless my eyes are playing tricks on me, I think Stevie has actually arrived."

Lisa wasn't the only person to see Stevie.

"Hey, there she is!" a voice cried. Then total confusion broke out.

Dozens of questions were thrown at Stevie before she was even close enough to hear them.

"Stevie, you've got to come over here!" someone yelled.

"Are we going to dress in costumes?" another voice asked.

Lisa and Carole ignored the uproar. They'd just spotted a couple of very familiar faces.

"Kate!" Carole cried. She ran to greet her friend.

"Christine!" Lisa shouted, waving furiously as she ran next to Carole.

"Italians!" Carole said, suddenly slowing.

"Wow!" Lisa said.

Stevie grinned proudly when she saw all that had been done to set up the fair while she'd been at the airport.

"You're all fantastic!" she announced, trying to be heard over the shouts of her friends and schoolmates.

"We need more staples!" one girl said.

"And blue crepe paper," a boy added.

"The booth I'm working on won't stay level because the ground's slanted," somebody complained.

"What are we supposed to do with all the Nerf balls?" another boy asked.

Stevie looked blank for a moment. "Nerf balls?"

"Which is going to be my booth?" someone else wanted to know.

"Yeah, we got a whole case of Nerf balls," the boy continued. "Are they prizes, or what?"

"Where *is* the hammer?" a girl wailed.

"Hold it, hold it," Stevie said with the voice of authority. "I'm here and I will answer all your questions. I have also brought reinforcements. Everybody, I want you to meet six friends of mine. Enrico, Marco, Andre, Gian, Kate and Christine. Every one of them is a master craftsman and can help us."

Stevie's classmates appeared skeptical.

"Any of you guys know anything about how to make a level booth on unlevel ground?" Stevie asked her reinforcements.

"Shims," Kate said promptly. "I'll help." She followed the person who was having trouble with the booth and tried to explain about props and shims as they walked.

Within a few minutes, Stevie had everybody assigned to a job. Enrico, it turned out, had been in charge of decorations for a horse fair in Italy and he had some ideas for what to do with the red and white crepe paper. He said blue wasn't necessary. Andre wanted to see how the booths were constructed, so he joined a crew who were about to assemble the next one. Christine agreed to help the boy who was setting up the archery booth. Stevie was pretty sure Christine was trying to keep a straight face at the idea. Gian agreed to help Lisa find some extra staples so they could put up more posters about the fair on their way to the shopping center, where they planned to buy more staples. Carole returned to her job of setting up the mini-bowling alley in the center booth.

Everybody seemed to have something to do except Stevie and Marco.

"Let me show you around here," Stevie said. She took him over to the oval course.

"And what's this for?" he asked, puzzled.

"That's where we're having the pony cart rides for the

kids in the hospital," Stevie explained. "Max has agreed to lend us the cart and ponies. Some of the kids may even be able to ride the ponies in a saddle. I don't know. Maybe it's crazy, but as far as I'm concerned, horseback riding has always been a way to make me forget my troubles. I just wanted to share that with these kids. Some of them have really big troubles—a lot bigger than mine ever were. Do you think I'm out of my mind?"

Marco smiled. "Maybe a little," he said. "But it's okay. You are a very generous person, Stevie. Everything you are doing here is for somebody else."

"Yeah," Stevie agreed, and without thinking, she added, "and her name is Veronica diAngelo."

"Who?"

"Oh, nothing. I mean, nobody," Stevie stammered.

Marco looked at her curiously, but he let it pass.

Fortunately, someone interrupted them right then. Somebody who looked very familiar was waving frantically to get Stevie's attention.

"I think we'd better get back," Stevie said. "Somebody seems to need me."

"Who is it?" Marco asked.

"I can't remember," Stevie said. "I've just forgotten his name." She squinted and tried hard to remember. "Oh, yes," she said. "It's Bobby Effingwell. He's the guy running against me for Middle School President."

Stevie waved back at Bobby and walked quickly to the

fairgrounds with Marco. When she got there, it turned out that Bobby wasn't the only one who needed to talk to her. A dozen questions awaited her. She was very pleased to find that she could supply a dozen answers in return. She turned to Bobby.

"Listen, my parents are making a big thing about this. I'm sorry to bother you," he said. Stevie decided right then and there that anyone as mousey as Bobby didn't have a chance of succeeding as Middle School President, much less winning the election. She hoped her face didn't betray her thoughts. "But my grandmother wants to hear my speech tomorrow and she can't get here by noon when we're supposed to go on," Bobby continued. "Can we do it later?"

Stevie's mind raced. Tomorrow was filled with activities and it all had to go like clockwork. Changing the time of something like that could cause problems. Still, maybe she could work something out.

"Let me think," she said. "The pony rides will be over by three-thirty. We could do it after that, say, at four?"

"Hey, great!" Bobby said. He dashed off to give the news to his parents. For a second, it crossed Stevie's mind that Bobby might have some political scheme in mind which made it more desirable for him to deliver his speech later in the day. But as she watched his receding figure wave gaily to his parents, she dismissed the thought. She had the feeling she was looking at a boy whose grandmother was going to see him lose badly in the school election. She was almost sorry she'd agreed to change the time of the speeches.

"And what's going on in your busy mind now?" Marco asked. Stevie had nearly forgotten he was there.

"I was just thinking about Bobby," she replied. "He's a nice boy, you know. He's so nice, he probably won't even resent me when I beat him in the election. Heck, he's so nice, he'll probably even vote for me." Marco laughed. "Come on. Let's get to work." Stevie returned her attention to the fair. "Do you know how to set up a ring-toss game?"

"Why don't you just show me what you want me to do and it will get done," Marco said.

"*Andiamo!*" Stevie said, leading the way.

"Oh, Stevie!" a voice called, interrupting them yet again. It was Veronica diAngelo, who had apparently gotten her voice back. "I've been looking all over for you!" she said sweetly. She spoke to Stevie, but her eyes were glued on Marco. Stevie wasn't surprised in the least.

"Well, here I am," Stevie said. "What can I do for you?"

"Oh, it's not what you can do for me. It's what *I* can do for *you*," Veronica cooed.

"Yes?" Stevie said.

"Well, I know you're working hard with all this fair business. I thought maybe the Italian boys would enjoy a little peace and quiet, perhaps over at my house?"

"Oh, but there's work to do," Marco said.

Veronica looked around her. For the first time she saw something other than Stevie and four good-looking boys. She saw that the four good-looking boys were working very hard on her school's Fair and her school's Hospital Festival.

"Work?" Veronica said, as if the word were unfamiliar to her. "You mean to tell me that Stevie has put you boys to *work*?" Her voice rose.

"I am going to make a ring-toss," Marco said proudly.

"I'm doing decorations," Enrico called down from a perilously high ladder. The red and white crepe paper he'd put up looked wonderfully festive.

"And Andre is in that booth over there," Marco said, pointing. "I think they are bolting it together. He's very good with such things, you know."

"But you're championship riders!" Veronica almost shrieked. "You shouldn't be doing these menial tasks! You should be—" She searched for words.

"What?" Marco asked. "We should be sitting on a veranda, sipping sodas and looking at a field of horses?"

That was obviously exactly what Veronica had in mind, particularly if the veranda overlooked her back yard.

"Pah! We can do that anywhere," Marco said, speaking for his friends. "We'd rather do something useful. And Stevie certainly needs us. Besides, it's fun to help with such worthwhile activities. Don't you agree?"

Veronica was cornered, and Stevie knew she couldn't

have done a better job of it herself. Veronica saw that she had only one route. She took it.

"Oh, yes," Veronica said. "I, myself, enjoy sipping soda on a veranda as much as the next person, and I would have been willing to do that with you boys if you'd wanted it. But since you don't, I can do something that is really much more important. I can help. After all, Fenton Hall is my school and I'm always willing to pitch in and do anything to help the school—or the poor little crippled children."

Stevie thought gleefully that she had never heard such insincere garbage in her life. It was music to her ears. All of the workers at the fair began to gather around Stevie and Veronica. This was a conversation they didn't want to miss.

"Why, how lovely of you, Veronica," Stevie responded, sweet as sugar. "We all know what your loyalty has meant to the school in the past." She paused for the insult to register on Veronica's face, but it was apparently too subtle for the girl to understand. Stevie went on. "We're almost finished here and I think I have all the volunteers I can use for this afternoon, but I do have one special job that you can do for me tomorrow at the fair."

"Me?" Veronica touched her chest to indicate herself, as if she wasn't sure who Stevie was talking to.

"It's a really important job, Veronica," Stevie said.

"Until now, I haven't found just the right person for it, but now I know who that is. It's you."

"Me?" she said again. Stevie thought Veronica ought to work a little more on her conversational techniques. She was getting really boring.

"Yes, you," Stevie said patiently. "You know, each one of these booths has an activity—ring-toss, bowling alley, all those things we do every year. Each booth needs at least one person to run that activity. Well, I want you to be in charge of Booth Number Thirteen tomorrow."

"Me?" Veronica repeated for the third time.

"No. Ghengis Khan," Stevie said, unable to hide her irritation any longer. "Of course, you. Anyway, I think Booth Thirteen is going to be our biggest attraction. You're just the person to run it."

"Well, I don't know, Stevie," Veronica began.

Stevie was afraid Veronica was going to back out of the project. "You *are,*" Stevie insisted. "After all, who cares more about Fenton Hall than you? Who has shown, year after year, that deep concern for the kids in the hospital? And, don't forget, this year, we've got horses involved. Is there anybody in town more involved in riding programs? Oh, yes, Veronica, this is an honor which you deserve."

"Well, I think you're flattering me a bit, Stevie," Veronica said. "But, of course, I do like to be a part—"

"Oh, you'll be a part of this," Stevie assured her. "An

important part. Well, I know you've had a tiring day, with all the work you've done on Garnet. I think you should relax. Tomorrow will take a lot out of you."

"I don't mind," Veronica told her. She was sounding very noble. Stevie tried to hide her own smile.

"Be here at eleven tomorrow," Stevie said. "And wear, you know, old clothes, something comfortable. It'll be a long day."

"Something like this old thing?" Veronica asked, pointing to the stylish brand-new outfit she was wearing.

"Exactly," Stevie said. "And remember—Booth Thirteen is all yours!"

"Oh, thanks, Stevie!" Veronica said. Stevie thought she sounded genuinely excited. "See you tomorrow!" She waved and left, no doubt heading for a veranda and a cold soda.

Lisa picked up a clipboard with the complete layout of the fairground. A puzzled look crossed her face.

"Stevie," she said. Stevie turned. "I don't get it. There *is* no Booth Thirteen."

Stevie's eyes danced. "There is now!" she said. "And, like I promised Veronica, it's going to be our main attraction and our biggest money-maker. Veronica has no idea of the wonderful sacrifice she's about to make for the glory of Fenton Hall!"

10

THE BIG DAY was bright, warm and beautiful. Stevie had known it would be. It was a perfect spring day, full of promise, only hinting of the muggy, hot summer to come.

Stevie donned her jeans and riding boots and a plaid shirt. Even if she wasn't planning to ride, these were the most comfortable clothes she owned. Besides, she thought there were probably people who wouldn't recognize her if she weren't wearing jeans!

Stevie extracted promises from all her brothers that they would come to the fair.

"Your father and I will be there, too," Mrs. Lake said.

"Of course you will be. You're my parents," she said,

remembering that Bobby Effingwell's grandmother would be in attendance as well.

Her mother hugged her and shooed her out the door.

By the time she arrived at the hospital grounds, she saw Lisa already there, with a clipboard in her hands, giving orders.

"Are you Stevie?" a boy asked Lisa, challenging her authority.

Ignoring the question, Lisa gave the boy an assignment. The boy snapped a quick salute and went to work.

"Nice job," Stevie said.

Lisa handed her the clipboard. "Everything is under control," she said. "Everything, that is, except this mysterious Booth Thirteen."

"That can wait for a few minutes," Stevie said. "We need Carole, Kate, and Christine to help with the final touches on that one. Here." She handed the clipboard back to Lisa. "I need to talk to somebody at the hospital. You keep this, and when the next person asks if you're me, just say yes, okay?"

"Sure thing," Lisa said.

Stevie walked into the entrance of the hospital. She'd talked to Miss Bellanger, the head nurse, quite a lot over the last few weeks to coordinate the project. Now it was time to make sure everything was on schedule.

Miss Bellanger was in her office when Stevie knocked on the door. "Hi," Stevie said. "Got a minute?"

"For anyone who can arrange to bring an entire school fair to my patients, with enough going on to entertain even the ones who can only watch from the window, I've got plenty of time," Miss Bellanger replied warmly.

"Not to mention the weather to go with it all," Stevie added.

"You're claiming credit for that, too?"

Stevie grinned. "Why not? Anyway, just to let you know, the ponies should be arriving about ten-thirty. Your kids are all welcome to come to our fair and they'll each get ten free tickets. At four o'clock, we've got school candidates' debates. That'll be boring for everybody, but by then your patients should be ready to return to their rooms. The way we've set this up, even the kids who can't participate can watch. I thought they'd rather watch than not. Is that right?"

"You've thought of everything, Stevie," Miss Bellanger said.

"Yes, I think I have," Stevie said, knowing full well that Miss Bellanger didn't understand the half of it. "Okay, see you later, then." In a minute, Stevie was back at the fairgrounds, ready for action.

"There you are, Stevie. What do you want us to do?" Carole asked. She, Kate, and Christine had just arrived.

A wicked gleam appeared in Stevie's eyes. "I want you to help me set up Booth Thirteen."

Lisa joined the group and Stevie began unfolding her plan.

"Christine, since you did such a great job on the T-shirts we wore at the rodeo, you're in charge of the sign for the booth. Here's what it's supposed to say." She handed Christine a piece of paper. Christine read it and her eyes lit up with amusement. "Lisa, you're artistic, so you can help Christine," Stevie added.

"Me, artistic?" Lisa sounded surprised.

"Well, you know where the paint is, don't you?" Stevie asked.

"I guess I'm *that* artistic. Let's go, Christine!" Lisa said, leading the way.

"Kate, here's a shopping list and some money," Stevie went on. "Did you see the little shopping center down the street? You can find everything we'll need in the housewares section of the supermarket."

"Outrageous!" Katie said, looking at her own list as Carole read over her shoulder. "Does Veronica know what's going on?"

"Veronica, as we all know, is devoted to the school and will do anything she can to help it and to entertain the— how did she put it?—'poor little crippled children,'" Stevie said innocently.

"Oh, yes. What a wonderful generosity of spirit that girl has," Kate said.

"What about me?" Carole asked.

"Well, you get the fun job of collecting the money. As soon as the sign goes up for Booth Thirteen, students from Fenton Hall are going to be lined up all the way back to the highway to get tickets. Sell them as fast as you can, okay? One of the Fenton Hall students will take over in a few minutes, but I'd like you to cover for now."

"Deal," Carole said. Stevie gave her a roll of tickets and a cash box. "I'll be fine," Carole said.

"It's going to be really busy," Stevie warned her.

"Oh, but it's all for such a good cause!" Carole said brightly.

Then Stevie and Carole heard a wonderful sound. It was the gentle clip-clop of ponies arriving.

"*Buon giorno!*" Enrico and Andre greeted Stevie and her friends cheerfully.

The carts, which were borrowed from Pine Hollow, were large enough to seat four or five children at once. There were two of them, and two ponies, also borrowed from Pine Hollow, named Nickel and Dime.

Stevie looked at her watch. It was ten-thirty exactly. Everything was going right on schedule.

* * *

CAROLE COULD HARDLY believe how smoothly everything was running. She wouldn't have thought a superwoman—let alone Stevie—would find a way to balance a hospital festival, a school fair, a political speech and six out-of-town visitors all in the same weekend. She was truly impressed with everything Stevie had accomplished.

"Hi, I'm Bobby Effingwell," a boy introduced himself, offering his hand. "I can take over at the cash box now," he said politely.

"Oh, sure," Carole told him. The name rang a bell, but she couldn't place it. Then she remembered who he was. He was Stevie's opponent for the Middle School Presidency. Carole studied his manner as he opened the cash box, pasted on a hopeful smile, and waited for his first customer.

"She'll win in a walk," Carole told herself.

"*Buon giorno!*" the four Italian boys greeted Carole from their pony carts. They looked wonderful. They were each wearing their formal riding clothes, which gave the little carts an official look. Since Carole had been relieved of her responsibilities at the cash box, she decided to join an activity more to her liking—namely, horses.

"Come on over this way," Carole called. She walked ahead of the carts and found a place for the boys to park them in the shade. As soon as the carts pulled to a halt, kids began appearing from the hospital.

Some were in pajamas and robes, and some were in jeans. A few of them were actually dressed up. There were three kids with crutches, five in wheelchairs and one lying flat on her back on a gurney. The kids who could walk best were pushing wheelchairs for those who couldn't. Some people might have thought that the one thing these kids had in common was that they were all sick. When Carole looked at them, she saw that what they all had in common was that they loved the ponies.

"What's his name?"

"Can I pat him?"

"Will he bite me?"

"Does he go fast?"

"Does he really like carrots?"

They had lots of questions and Carole sensed that all of them were eager to have a chance to ride in the carts and hug the ponies.

"I think we're going to have to get to work here, boys," Carole told Enrico, Marco, Andre, and Gian. With that, they looked to see how they were going to load the kids into the pony carts under the supervision of Miss Bellanger, who had come to help.

It was a tricky business. The carts hadn't been designed with wheelchairs, casts, and crutches in mind. Carole found a way to do it all with the help of her Italian crew. They fashioned a ramp from some boards to make it easier for the kids to get into the carts. The kids were both eager and patient. Carole found that their patience was rewarded. Looking at their faces, she knew that it didn't matter what problems the kids were taking up the ramp with them. Those problems were all left behind once they were strapped into the cart. For once, they were just children, having fun in a pony cart.

The Italian boys were having a blast, too. Each cart had one Italian equestrian champion with the reins in his hand and another walking ahead of the cart, leading the way. The children loved their glamorous outfits and their formal manner. They even loved their Italian accents.

"Hey, can you sing *Santa Lucia?*" one of the children asked. "We learned it in school last year when we were studying Marco Polo and Venice. Don't all the gondoliers in Venice sing *Santa Lucia* all the time?"

Marco grinned. Clearly, he enjoyed challenges. "All the time," he assured the boy. "And since my name is also Marco, you know I must be from Venice—" Carole knew this was a fib. Marco was actually from Florence. "—so my friends and I will sing for you," Marco finished.

At once, all four of the Italian boys began singing *Santa Lucia*. It took them a while to pick a key they all liked and two of them didn't seem very familiar with the words, but a couple of the children knew them in English and joined along.

"What's going on over here?" Stevie asked Carole,

drawn to the course by the strange, more or less musical, sounds. "Did somebody's dog get sick?"

"Oh, no, it's just our Italian guests, being pony cart singers, or something like that," Carole said.

Stevie stood by her and watched for a few minutes. Seeing the children smile and sing and enjoy themselves made her feel warm and happy inside. Carole put her arm across Stevie's shoulder and gave her a hug. "You're a miracle worker, you know," she said.

"It's not me," Stevie said. "It's them." She gestured toward the carts as they circled the field.

"Do you mean the ponies, the carts, the children, or the Italian boys?" Carole asked.

"All of it," Stevie said.

Carole thought she was right.

11

"THE CHILDREN ARE having a wonderful time, aren't they?" Kate asked Stevie.

"Yes, and so are our Italian visitors," she said. "It's great to listen to them. But I think the most fun of all is about to come. Has Christine finished the sign?"

"Yes. They put it up about five minutes ago. Look, there's already a line by the cash box," Kate pointed out.

Stevie grinned wickedly. "This is a dream come true."

And at that moment, the fair's star attraction arrived.

"Good morning, Stevie," Veronica said. "Where are our foreign guests?" she asked, eagerly turning her head.

"Over there, with the pony carts," Stevie replied.

"You have them working again?" Veronica asked.

"Well, Veronica, they were so inspired by your devotion to the cause of the children and the school that they just insisted on helping out," Stevie said smoothly.

"Oh. Well, I guess I'm ready. Where's Booth Thirteen?" Veronica wanted to know.

"This way," Stevie said. This was a tricky moment. She had to make it impossible for Veronica to back out and the only way she could do that was to make it more embarrassing for her to leave than to stay. "Hey, everybody!" Stevie announced. "Veronica's here! She's our star attraction and will definitely be our biggest money-maker."

The students gathered around. As if somebody had cued them, they cheered. Veronica smiled graciously.

"You know, Veronica," Stevie continued. "Last year the fair made almost a thousand dollars. This year, our goal is to make even more. We're hoping for fifteen hundred dollars. With your help, I know we can do it."

"Me? I'm just trying to pitch in, Stevie," Veronica said, doing a poor job of acting humble. It was done. Stevie had cornered her.

"Well, here's your booth," Stevie said, taking Veronica by the elbow. "Lucky Number Thirteen!"

And there it was. Stevie couldn't keep her eyes off Veronica as she read the sign.

SOGGY NERF BALL TOSS
Throw a soggy Nerf ball!
Hit Veronica diAngelo!
Win prizes!
Three Throws for One Ticket!

There was a bucket of water and a case of Nerf balls at the front counter. At the back of the booth was a lone seat where Veronica would serve as a target.

Behind them, Stevie and Veronica heard kids clamoring for their turn.

"I'm first!"

"No, me! I've been waiting longer!"

"Let me have a try!"

It seemed that everybody who knew Veronica wanted a shot at her.

Veronica glared at Stevie. For the second time in as many days, she appeared to be speechless.

"I'm telling you, Veronica. A long line formed for tickets the minute the sign went up. You, and you alone, are going to put us over fifteen hundred dollars," Stevie said.

"Stevie, they'll hit me and get me wet," Veronica hissed.

"Don't worry," Stevie assured her. "Most of these kids don't have good aim. And, after all, a lot of them are going to be, er—what did you call them?—the 'little crippled children' from the hospital. They probably won't get anywhere near you."

"I'm going to do this, you know," Veronica said. "And then I will never speak to you again."

That was exactly what Stevie had been hoping for.

*　　*　　*

SOON AFTER BOOTH Thirteen opened up for business, all the other booths opened as well. The fair began at eleven o'clock and by eleven-thirty, the entire fairground was bustling with activity. Stevie checked all the booths. They had found the wooden rings which had been missing earlier at the ring-toss. The Magic Wishing Tree had all its prize claims stapled on correctly. The fortune teller had polished her crystal ball and memorized her list of "fortunes." The bowling alley had set up all ten pins, instead of the six somebody had put up by mistake. The red and white decorations looked bright and cheerful. Everywhere Stevie went, her schoolmates, riding friends, and the children from the hospital were having a wonderful time. The loudest cheering noises came from Booth Thirteen and from the pony cart track.

Stevie found herself standing under a tree in the middle of the fairground, soaking it all in. She closed her eyes and listened. Everywhere, there were sounds of success. People were having fun. The fair was making money for the school. She'd done it. She had actually pulled off everything she'd been assigned to do—almost.

The things that hadn't been accomplished yet were the campaign speeches and debates and the Italian boys' riding demonstration. It was too bad that she was going to have to miss that demonstration in the afternoon, but there was no way she could leave the fairground until the fair was finished and cleaned up. She'd get a chance to see their performance the next day at Pine Hollow.

Now, there was only one thing she wanted to make the day complete.

"Hi there, beautiful."

The one thing she wanted had appeared. Phil Marston had arrived.

"You think flattery will get you anywhere!" she said, pretending to be annoyed.

"Not really," Phil said. "I'm just hoping that if I make a big play for the person in charge of this event, it might get me to the head of the line at Booth Thirteen. You wouldn't happen to be responsible for that wonderful idea, would you?"

"Me?" Stevie asked innocently.

Phil laughed and gave her a hug. "So, what can I do?" he asked.

"Hmmmm," Stevie said thoughtfully. "You know, I've been meaning to try the ring-toss. Let's get some tickets and see who's better."

"Okay," Phil agreed. "The winner gets to serve as pitching coach over at Booth Thirteen!"

"You're on!"

"HI. WHAT'S YOUR name?" Carole asked. She was speaking to the girl about her own age who was on the gurney by the pony carts.

"Marie," the girl responded glumly.

"I don't know if we can get this rig into a cart safely," Carole began.

"You can't," Marie said. *She's probably right,* Carole thought, but there was something about Marie's tone of voice that bothered her. Carole felt as if somebody had just slammed a door in her face. And somehow, Carole didn't believe that Marie's situation was that hopeless.

"What are you in for?" Carole asked.

Marie seemed a little irritated. "I have a fractured pelvis," she said. "And in case that's not enough, both my legs are broken, too. Don't ask if you can sign my cast, okay? It's not funny."

"I didn't say it was," Carole retorted. She decided to try again. "Would you like to pat one of the ponies?" she asked.

"No."

"So how come you're here?" Carole asked.

"Because Miss Bellanger said it would make me feel better."

"You're going to make this very hard, aren't you?" Carole asked. It was only after she'd said it that Carole realized how harsh she sounded.

But it worked. "I'm sorry," Marie said. "Miss Bellanger tells me I have a way of taking my anger out on everybody else. I know you're just trying to be nice, but, believe me, it doesn't really help."

"That's fair." Carole nodded. "Listen, I've got to help

the next batch of kids into the cart. Would you like me to ask Miss Bellanger to take you back inside now?"

Marie was quiet for a moment. She seemed to be thinking over Carole's offer. "No, thanks," she said. "I'll stick around."

"Okay," Carole said and turned her attention to the others. She didn't want to let one person who was determined to be miserable ruin the day for the others.

"My turn! My turn!" said a little boy. Marco picked him up and put him into the pony cart. Once the boy was strapped in, he knew exactly what to tell his driver: "*Andiamo!*" The cart lurched forward and the singing began once again.

SPLAT! SQUISH! THUMP!

"Oh, no, I missed."

"Here, try again. Aim higher this time!"

"You're not allowed to duck!" someone called to Veronica.

"I am too!" she yelled.

The action at Booth Thirteen was never-ending and Stevie enjoyed every minute of it. She went on an inspection of the other booths. She helped restock the food booth with popcorn and candy apples. She took over temporarily at the balloon dartboard when the student working there needed to take a break. She solved problems, she gave directions, and she answered questions.

She watched as Carole and the Italian boys kept the pony carts going. The shrieks of laughter from that section of the fair were delightful. It was nice to have some of the hospital patients participating in their school fair. Somehow, everything was working.

Stevie wandered over to the table where tickets were being sold.

"How are sales?" she asked.

"Brisk," came the answer from one of the student cashiers.

"Oh, yes. You've done a wonderful job here," said the other cashier. It was Bobby Effingwell, Stevie's opponent in the school election. "You know, you surprised me," Bobby said. "When somebody told me I'd be running against you, I thought it would be easy. Nobody could believe that Stevie Lake could actually do something serious or take on a lot of responsibility. But you've proven me wrong, Stevie. I think you'll probably win the election, and that's great. You deserve it. I just want you to promise me one thing."

Stevie wasn't sure she was hearing Bobby correctly. If she'd been in his place, she'd be mad as a hornet at her opponent. He was being downright gracious.

"Sure, Bobby. What is it?" she asked.

"Promise me that when you do other projects like these as Middle School President, you'll let me help you. I really want to be part of these things," Bobby replied.

Stevie was even more surprised by that remark. It had never occurred to her that being President of the Middle School meant doing this kind of thing a lot.

"There are a lot more events coming up," Bobby continued, "like the school cookie sale, the canned goods drive, and the book drive. I want to be right there in the middle of it all, okay?"

"Sure," Stevie agreed. "You'll be there. It's a promise."

"One more thing," Bobby said. She nodded. "Can you cover for me here for a few minutes?" he asked. "I just have to get over to Booth Thirteen. I've bought ten tickets, see . . ."

"Be my guest!" Stevie said, laughing. She wouldn't have thought sweet Bobby had it in him. "And throw one for me, okay?"

They shook hands, and he left.

By the time Bobby reappeared, claiming triumph with the soggy Nerf balls, Stevie's family had arrived and she wanted to give them the grand tour. She looked at her watch. She couldn't believe it was already after three o'clock. The pony carts were almost done for the day. Some of the booths were getting ready to close up, particularly the popcorn booth, which had sold out of everything. It was nearly time for the speeches.

Stevie could tell that her parents were very impressed with what she'd done. She had had the ability to surprise her parents a number of times in her life, but rarely with something they were proud of.

Her brothers might have told her what a great job she'd done except that all three of them were waiting in the line at Booth Thirteen! Stevie was almost beginning to feel sorry for Veronica. Her older brother, Chad, was a pitcher on the Junior Varsity softball team at Fenton. He was good. He wouldn't miss.

Stevie took her parents over to the bowling alley, where Phil had somehow been talked into taking over as pin-setter. For a second, she asked herself how she had managed to con so many of her friends into working so hard. Then she decided that some questions shouldn't be asked.

When Stevie looked at her watch again, it was three-thirty. That meant it was time to close down the pony carts so the Italian boys could get back to Pine Hollow in time for their demonstration. She helped the last load of children out of the carts, patted the ponies herself, and sent them on their way.

"I'm sorry I can't be there," she told Enrico. "Tell the others, too. But I'll be there tomorrow. Okay?"

"It's okay, Stevie," Enrico said. "We know you've been awfully busy today. We understand."

"You've been pretty busy, too," Stevie said. "Have I worked you too hard?"

"Work? No, this has been wonderful fun. How else

would I have known what an awful singing voice Marco has?" Enrico smiled and waved his pony whip gently, urging Nickel to return to Pine Hollow.

Stevie waved to all four boys, wondering if there was any real way to thank them for all they had done for her.

There was a moment of quiet, Stevie's first all day. She leaned against a tree, enjoying the cool shade, and breathed deeply, sighing as she let out the air.

"Tired?" someone asked. It was Phil.

"I guess I am," Stevie said.

"You've worked awfully hard today. You've done a lot."

"That's for sure," Stevie agreed. "But everything worked out. Can you believe it?"

"Yes, I can," Phil said. "You have this way of taking on an outrageous job and somehow succeeding. It's one of the things I like about you."

"Not the only one, I hope," Stevie said, looking into his deep green eyes. "Because, I promise you, I will never, *ever* again take on this much at one time in my whole entire life!"

"Just talk," Phil teased.

"Just you see," Stevie said. And for once, she meant it.

12

IT WAS THREE fifty-five.

All of the booths except Number Thirteen were closed down. The last customer took a last toss at Veronica. She ducked unsuccessfully one last time.

"Quitting time!" Stevie announced, freeing Veronica from the torture of the day.

"So soon?" Veronica asked icily.

There was nothing to say to that. Stevie handed Veronica a towel and watched as she disappeared toward her home. Stevie almost felt sorry for her. Almost.

The crowd was heading for the platform, where the fair program had promised the school speeches and debates would take place. Stevie walked in that direction as well, and as she did so, she scanned the people milling around.

Where were Lisa and Carole? What had happened to Kate and Christine? Why didn't she see Phil anywhere? Then she remembered the Italian boys' riding demonstration. They must have all decided that that was more exciting than listening to her speech. She tried to hide her disappointment, but it wasn't easy. If she'd ever needed friends, she needed them now. *After all,* she told herself, *I have to wait until tomorrow to see the demonstration. Why don't they? What's the Saddle Club about? Aren't you supposed to help and support your friends when they need you?*

"Whoa," she told herself. It didn't make sense to get upset about something she couldn't change. After all, she was about to deliver an important speech.

She reached into her right-hand back pocket, feeling for the comfortable lump of paper that she'd spent so many evenings scribbling on lately. It was her speech.

There was no comfortable lump.

She smiled encouragement to herself. Of course there was a lump of paper. She just hadn't put it in her right-hand back pocket. She must have put it in her left-hand back pocket.

She reached into her left-hand back pocket. Still no lump. Then she began to get worried. She checked her front pockets. She started to check her shirt pockets until she realized the shirt she was wearing didn't have pockets. Her speech was nowhere to be found.

Stevie took another deep breath. She felt terribly

alone. Her friends had left without saying anything, and now she didn't even have her speech to reassure her.

She looked around, hoping for comfort. All she could see were about a hundred schoolmates and their families. Every one of them was headed for the place where they were expecting to see Stevie, the new Stevie of the new leaf, pull one more rabbit out of one more hat. All she had to do was to work one more, final miracle of the day. Could she do it?

She'd worked on the speech for so long that every phrase was familiar to her. Could she remember it standing in front of more than a hundred people?

Well, she'd have to try, or else she'd have to think up something entirely new to say on the spot. Stevie's mind began racing as she proceeded to the platform.

The whole day, and the three and a half weeks leading up to it, flashed through her mind. It had been quite a time. Even with a lot of help from her friends, she'd seen her grades slip a bit and she'd had to skip a couple of riding classes. No doubt about it, she didn't want to go through a period like that again. Of course, the experience had had its rewards, too. For one thing, she was having a lot of fun spending time with the Italian boys, and she had most definitely gotten the best of Veronica diAngelo. Most important, however, the Festival had been a wonderful success for Children's Hospital and the Fair had made a lot of money for her school. She hadn't counted the proceeds yet, but she was pretty sure they'd exceeded their $1,500 goal. Stevie's new leaf had been a lot of work, but it was worth it. The question was, would her leaf stay turned for good?

Stevie sat where Miss Fenton indicated and tried to remember what it was she wanted to say. The only good news at that moment was that Bobby was supposed to go first.

He stood up and the crowd became quiet. Stevie saw his parents in the front row. His grandmother was there. She waved to him.

"Good afternoon," he began. "I'm here to try to convince you to vote for me for Middle School President and I've got to say it's not going to be an easy thing to do, not after the show Stevie Lake has put on for us all today."

The crowd laughed. Stevie found herself feeling vaguely uncomfortable. After all, those people out there didn't know that the biggest reason she had done any of this was because of Veronica diAngelo and four Italian boys. She shifted in her seat and tried to smile.

Bobby went on. He had prepared a good, thoughtful speech. He had a lot of proposals for the Middle School, including ideas for several community projects, canned goods drives, and book drives. He explained that he had always been on committees at school and wanted to be helpful to the students as well as to the town.

Stevie listened. Bobby Effingwell cared. He really

cared. He was earnest, sincere, and hardworking. She'd hardly ever talked to him, but she found that she could really admire the boy who was giving the speech she was hearing. Stevie began to feel a little rotten about how confident she'd been about winning the election. Life just wasn't that simple.

While she was listening attentively, Stevie saw something out of the corner of her eye that she could hardly believe. It was Max's truck, pulling a four-horse van. As soon as it drew to a stop, Christine, Kate, Carole, and Lisa piled out, as well as Phil, Enrico, Marco, Andre and Gian. They began unloading horses and equipment from the van. Stevie couldn't believe what she was seeing, but she knew it was true. Her friends had decided to move the demonstration from Pine Hollow over to the hospital. It was a great idea that had never occurred to her!

Stevie's thoughts were interrupted by polite applause. Bobby stepped back to his chair and sat down. Stevie reached over, took his hand, and pumped it.

"You're something," she said. Bobby looked at her curiously.

"Stevie Lake," Miss Fenton announced.

Stevie gulped. For a second, her entire body shook. She was very, very nervous, but she knew what she had to do. She saw her Saddle Club friends and the Italian boys join the audience, standing at the back. She took a deep breath, stood up, and walked toward the audience. She was ready.

"This has been quite a day," she began. "I guess you all don't know it, but I had no idea what I was getting myself into when I agreed to do all these things. I'm such a dummy, I didn't even realize they were all happening on the same day!" People laughed. Stevie wasn't sure why. She wasn't trying to be funny. "Anyway, the day is here and mostly over now and there are a few things I have to say. First of all, I want to thank my friends. I couldn't have gotten through the day, and you wouldn't have had such a good time, without them. That goes for all my classmates who worked so hard and for some other friends who don't even go to Fenton Hall. In case you think that group has finished working, you should see what I see, too. Right after my speech, you're all invited to go over to the pony cart course, where you'll see one outstanding demonstration of riding by an international team of riders, better known to all of you as the Singing Pony Carters!"

Everybody looked over their shoulders to see what was happening.

"But the other thing I want to say," Stevie continued impulsively, "is what a terrific person Bobby Effingwell is. All day, he worked hard selling tickets. He never complained. He just did the job. He told me how much it meant to him to be involved. Well, I think Bobby is involved and I think he ought to stay involved. He told me he hoped I would ask him to help on other projects that I run. But, Bobby, you've got that backwards. I'm not good at running projects. I'm only good at getting my friends to do things. You're the one who's good at running things. I think you should have a chance at running the student government of the Middle School."

Stevie was astonished to hear the words coming from her mouth. But they were absolutely right. Bobby would be perfect. He'd do the job right and he deserved it. Besides, she would never make it in a job like that. One more bottle of glue spread out under one more teacher's shoes and she'd be out of the job anyway.

She was ready to finish her speech then. "I'm going to vote for Bobby Effingwell, and I think that all of you should, too."

The first person to stand up and start clapping was Miss Fenton. Stevie was pleased to see that the next was Bobby's grandmother. Then her own parents joined the ovation. Pretty soon, everybody was standing up and cheering. They were cheering for Bobby and they were cheering for Stevie. The cheers for Stevie were for all the good things she had done. The cheers for Bobby were for what he would do as President of the Middle School.

"All right now," Stevie said. "Enough of this political stuff. Let's get back to fun things—the horses!"

With that, the entire crowd moved over to the pony cart area for the demonstration.

Stevie wanted to go over there right away, but there was something else she had to do first.

She dashed into the hospital and found Miss Bellanger in her office. "There's one more thing," she said. "There's going to be a riding demonstration in a few minutes. I bet a lot of the patients would like to see that, too. Can you get them to the windows?"

"A riding demonstration?" Miss Bellanger said. "Do I recall authorizing that?"

"Well, not exactly," Stevie said. "But I promise you, it will be neat. The kids will love it."

Miss Bellanger sighed. "Like I said, Stevie. You think of everything." She reached for the microphone to the P.A. system and made an announcement. All Stevie heard of it before she raced out the door was, "Your attention please. We have more good news, courtesy of the indomitable Stevie Lake—"

"THEY'RE JUST AS good as we thought, aren't they?" Carole asked Stevie as the two of them stood and watched the Italian boys do their demonstration.

"Absolutely," Stevie said.

"How do they get their horses to do those things?" Lisa asked.

"Training," Kate supplied.

The four boys were working through intricate patterns with their horses. Some of the riding was a little like the drill work that Stevie, Lisa, and Carole had practiced, though the boys were much better than they had been. A lot of their performance was a dressage demonstration, in quadruplicate.

The four riders lined up and began walking their horses toward the far end of the oval. At an invisible signal, all four horses began prancing, in step with one another.

"How can they do that with untrained horses? I mean, those guys have never ridden on those horses before!" Carole said, obviously envious.

"The horses may not be trained to do that, but the riders are," Max said. "The riders are just talking to their horses with their legs, hands, and seat. Isn't it wonderful?"

"Yes," Kate agreed.

At the far end of the oval, the formation changed. All four horses returned to the center and then each went to a separate corner, forming a square. At an invisible signal, they began cantering toward the center of the ring, and somehow, miraculously, managed to cross one another without running in to each other. The audience applauded. The horses reversed directions at the corners and repeated the exercise.

"Amazing," Christine said.

"Could we ever do something like that?" Lisa asked Max.

"Sure," Max replied, "but first you have to learn to keep your heels down, toes in, hands steady, and—"

"I know, eyes straight ahead," Lisa finished for him. "I guess he means first things first," she said to Kate. Kate nodded.

By then, the boys had started a zigzag pattern so complicated that Stevie wished she were in a hot air balloon so she could see it more clearly. What was clear from where she was, however, was that they really knew what they were doing. They proceeded flawlessly through the entire exercise.

"Fabulous!" she exclaimed when they completed the set.

"Outstanding!" Phil said. They both clapped loudly.

Then, with the horses once again responding to imperceptible signals, the riders began a snaking pattern that turned out to be a figure eight. They cantered their horses through the figure. The work was so precise that it appeared the riders would run into each other every time they crossed the intersection in the middle of the eight, but no such thing happened. The boys were too good.

"Boy, and I had them driving pony carts!" Stevie moaned. "They must think I'm a jerk!"

"Nobody thinks you're a jerk," Phil assured her. "In fact, now I think they're going to do something special here just for you."

As Phil spoke, Stevie looked up and saw that all four horses and riders were approaching her straight on. Stevie wondered what was happening. The crowd did, too.

The horses drew to a halt just a few feet in front of her.

Then, while Stevie watched breathlessly, all four horses inched their front legs forward, lowering themselves into a bow to her—just her.

"Oh," Stevie said.

"Oooooh," the crowd agreed.

And when the horses rose back up again, everybody burst into applause for the Italian equestrian team, and for Stevie.

What a day it was!

13

"DID SOMEBODY PACK up the Nerf balls?" Stevie asked later that afternoon.

"Better than that," Phil told her. "After the booth closed, we sold them as souvenirs—and made a wicked profit!"

Stevie was sitting in the den in her own house, lounging in her father's recliner. She had a glass of iced tea in one hand and a bowl of popcorn close by the other. But she wasn't paying much attention to either of these luxuries. Her mind was still racing over potentially unfinished business from the very full day she'd just had on the hospital grounds. She was discovering that, thanks to the friends who surrounded her, there really was no unfinished business.

"And the games?" she asked.

"All packed and stored back at Fenton, along with the dismantled booths," Carole assured her.

"Did all the horses and their equipment get safely back to Pine Hollow?" Stevie wanted to know.

"Every bit of it," Marco promised her. "The horses have been groomed, fed, and watered, and are now enjoying a much-deserved rest. You should learn from them and begin enjoying this party your mother planned for you."

Stevie smiled. While she had been working on the final matters of the day, her mother had invited her best friends over to their house to celebrate Stevie's defeat in the school election. She felt good about everything that had happened that day, especially turning the election over to Bobby Effingwell.

"He'll do a good job. I know it," Stevie had told her mother.

"Yes, he will," she'd agreed. "You did the right thing, you know." Then she'd hugged Stevie.

"I know," Stevie had said, hugging her back.

"PIZZA'S HERE!" MRS. Lake called down the stairs to the den, where all ten fair-givers were having their celebration. "I need somebody to help with the boxes!"

Instantly, she had five volunteers, more than enough for the four pizzas. The fifth person brought down a case of cold soda.

"Ah, the perfect American meal," Stevie joked, watching her Italian guests arrive in the den with pizza. "Do you have anything like this at home?" she teased.

Marco and Andre began opening the boxes to see just what it was they were carrying. They shook their heads. "No," they said. "We have something by the same name, but it isn't anything like this at all," Marco told her. "What is all this?"

"Food," Stevie said simply. She felt too exhausted to try to explain. Phil took over the job. The Italians were quite interested to find things like hamburger and bacon on the pizzas.

"No, I have never seen anything like it at all," Gian announced finally. He took a bite. "But I hope I see something like it a lot more!"

"As long as you're in America, you'll see plenty of it," Kate promised them all.

Stevie took a bite and thought about what Kate had just said. It reminded her of something that was bothering her a little bit.

"Speaking of what you're going to see in America," Stevie said to the boys. "I'm sorry that I haven't been doing such a good job as a tour guide."

"You seem to have enough jobs as it is. Do you really want to take on another now?" Enrico teased.

"Well, but you're here, you know, and there are things you should see—" Stevie began.

"Ah, yes," said Marco. "The grand tour." He said it as if it were a title: The Grand Tour. "We travel a lot as a team, you know. And we have been taken on a lot of tours. Everybody has a list of favorite sights. You wouldn't believe some of the things we've had to look at. In one place, in the middle of summer, somebody went ten miles out of their way to show us where the toboggan run was in the winter!"

Stevie recalled that a toboggan run had figured on her original suggestion list. She smiled weakly.

"Well, what about Washington, D.C.?" she asked a little defensively. "I mean, there's the White House and the Washington Monument and the Smithsonian and the Capitol—"

"We saw it all on our last visit here," Andre explained. "We were staying in the city and we saw everything. We found that being a tourist in Washington is more exhausting than riding—"

"You mean you don't want to go into the city?" Stevie interrupted.

The boys looked at one another uncomfortably. Clearly, they didn't want to hurt anybody's feelings. "Well, to tell you the truth, we'd rather spend time with friends our own age. We can learn more about your country eating pizza and drinking soda than we can from a tour bus."

"Really?" Stevie asked.

"Really," Gian said sincerely, and the other boys nodded.

"Wonderful!" Stevie said, clapping with delight. "I'd much rather stay here tomorrow morning than go on the four-hour tour I talked my father into taking with us."

"We don't want to disappoint him," Marco said.

"You won't disappoint him. You'll thrill him," Stevie said. "So what would you like to do instead?"

"Tomorrow is tomorrow and there's no need to decide yet," Andre said. "But right now, we are all wondering about something. Do you mind if we ask you about it?"

"No, what is it?" the Americans responded eagerly.

"Can you show us how to dance like Americans do?"

"Absolutely!" Stevie cried. It took only a few minutes to push back the chairs and clear a dance space. Stevie turned on the stereo and began selecting music for the dance demonstration. At the first sounds of music, the dancing began.

CAROLE STOOD WITH her hands on her hips, watching Marco as he tried to dance the way she had.

"No, no," she said. "You've got to loosen up, feel the music and move with it."

Marco tried again. His dancing was a little better, but not much.

"Stop flapping your arms," Carole said.

Marco laughed. "I guess I'm awful at this," he said.

"Not really. It's just that you don't have the feel of it. It must be the way I'm describing it." Carole thought for a second. "Wait a minute. I've got it. Think of yourself as riding on a horse. You know how you have to move with the motion of the horse? Now, pretend you're on a horse that's cantering, and—Hey, I think you're getting it!"

"Yes, I can feel it. I don't look so silly now, right?"

"Right!" Carole said. She began dancing along with him.

"But I don't understand," Gian said to Christine. They were sitting in the chairs by the dance area having a serious conversation. Neither of them felt like dancing. Both preferred to talk.

"Why do your people call themselves Native Americans now?"

Christine smiled. "Your own Christopher Columbus is the one who called us Indians," she said. "He may have been a courageous man and a brilliant navigator—after all, he knew how to get here. He just didn't know where he'd gotten. He thought he was in India and assumed we were Indians. My people have been named after a mistake for five hundred years. It's time to correct the mistake."

"So now the western movies will be called 'cowboys and Native Americans?'" he teased.

"Why not?" Christine countered.

"I guess you're right," he said. "Now, tell me about Western riding—"

"YOU'RE A REALLY good dancer!" Andre said, watching Kate as she moved to the music on the stereo.

"I always exercise to rock music," she said. "I've got a pretty good collection, too. And now that I'm living on a dude ranch, I'm also starting a country and western collection, but it's not so good for exercise."

"What's different about country and western music?" Andre asked.

"IT'S A SLOW one, Stevie. Want to dance with me?" Phil asked. He offered her a hand. She took it and let him help pull her up out of the lounge chair. Then he wrapped his arms around her and held her close. Stevie loved dancing with Phil, especially the slow dances. She put her head on his shoulder. They moved easily to the music.

"You're amazing," he said softly to her. "You did more today than a lot of people do in a lifetime. It was a little weird, though. Every time I turned around, there was somebody else saying how much work you had done and how good it was. I mean, I've always known you're special, but what you accomplished today was unbelievable."

"I couldn't have done it without my friends, like you," she murmured. He hugged her.

*   *   *

"SO, HOW DO you make the horses do all that?" Lisa asked Enrico. "I never saw anything like what you guys did this afternoon. I don't mean I haven't seen a good dressage exhibition. I have. I saw Dorothy DeSoto do a program. But all four of you were doing it at the same time. I know it didn't have anything to do with the horses because I ride those same horses. They're good, all right, but they haven't had any special training. How does it work?"

"You want to know our secrets?"

"Are they secret?" Lisa asked. It hadn't occurred to her that she was prying.

Enrico smiled. "Not to you, Lisa. Not to you and your friends. Now look," he began. "It's in the legs. The horse needs to know that you know what you are doing so that if you make the slightest change in the position of your legs, he will respond."

"All in your legs?" Lisa asked to make sure.

"Well, not exactly. It's in your seat, too. And, of course, your hands."

Lisa thought for a few seconds about what he'd said. It sounded awfully familiar. Then she realized why. She'd heard it dozens of times from Max! "That's how it is with all riding," Lisa said. "That's no secret."

"Just so!" Enrico said. "I knew you would understand. Now, shall we dance?"

"Sure," Lisa said. "And I'll promise to teach you all the

secrets of American dances. See, it's all in the legs. And the feet. And the hips. Oh, yes, and the arms."

Grinning, Enrico offered her his hand and they joined the others on the dance floor.

PHIL LOOKED DOWN at the top of Stevie's head, resting on his shoulder. They moved slowly to the music.

"I think my favorite part of today was Veronica at Booth Thirteen. That was a stroke of genius, Stevie. Of course, what you did for Bobby Effingwell was probably even better. You could have beaten him in the election, but the fact is, he'll do a good job. And he'll have a better time doing it. You'd get tired of being a goody-goody and he was born that way, wasn't he, Stevie? Stevie?"

She didn't answer him. She was fast asleep.

"I CAN'T BELIEVE they're gone already," Stevie said sadly. "It seems like they just got here yesterday."

Stevie was talking about the Italian boys. She and the other four members of The Saddle Club were sitting in a crowded booth at TD's on Tuesday afternoon. They'd just finished a class at Pine Hollow and were having a meeting.

"But wasn't it great having them here?" Lisa asked. "We learned so much from them."

"I think they learned a lot from us, too," Christine said.

"That reminds me. What were you and Gian talking about so seriously on Saturday night at Stevie's?" Carole asked.

"Oh, things," Christine answered evasively. Then she smiled.

"I guess we know the answer to that!" Kate joked.

"Well, you and Andre seemed to be having a pretty good time, too!" Christine countered.

"Actually, we were," Kate said. "We found we had a few things in common."

"Liking each other, you mean?" Lisa asked.

"I guess so," Kate admitted. "Anyway, he promised to send me postcards from all the places they visit.

"Speaking of getting along, Carole," Kate said. "You certainly managed to show Marco some moves on the dance floor!"

"He found he had a natural talent for American dancing," Carole said. "I just helped him discover it, with the help of a few horseback riding hints."

"Are you going to explain that?" Stevie asked.

"No." Carole grinned. "Let's just say, we had fun."

"You all did," Stevie said.

"You did, too," Lisa said.

"Maybe." Stevie shrugged. "I just don't remember much of it. Phil told me I fell asleep while we were dancing. Can you believe it?"

"Considering how tired you were that night, I believe it," Kate said.

The waitress arrived with their orders. She delivered two fudge sundaes, one on vanilla ice cream, one on mint chocolate chip, a caramel sundae on vanilla, and a strawberry sundae on strawberry, all with maraschino cherries on top. "Now, let me see. Who ordered the banana ice cream with blackberry syrup, marshmallow topping, walnuts—"

"That's me," Stevie said.

"I never would have guessed," the waitress said. "Here you go." She put the dish in front of Stevie and walked away.

"She's getting better, you know," Stevie said. "She used to slap my dish down and run away. Now she just walks. That's progress."

"You are one of a kind, Stevie," Christine said.

"And we wouldn't have it any other way," Lisa added.

"Because who could stand more than one friend like Stevie?" Carole finished.

"Friends!" Stevie said, grinning. "You're all just wonderful. Oh, and speaking of wonderful. I got the greatest idea today at riding class. We're going to be having our first pony club rally next week and I thought that maybe it might be fun to plan a sort of fund-raising picnic beforehand. You know, we could set up some booths and games, do some sort of demonstration. It wouldn't be too much work. If you could all pitch in—"

Four maraschino cherries hit Stevie at the same time.

ABOUT THE AUTHOR

BONNIE BRYANT is the author of more than forty books for young readers, including novelizations of movie hits such as *Teenage Mutant Ninja Turtles* and *Honey, I Shrunk the Kids,* written under her married name, B. B. Hiller.

Ms. Bryant began writing The Saddle Club in 1986. Although she had done some riding before that, she intensified her studies then and found herself learning right along with her characters Stevie, Carole, and Lisa. She claims that they are all much better riders than she is.

Ms. Bryant was born and raised in New York City. Her husband and sometime coauthor, Neil Hiller, died in 1989. She lives in Greenwich Village with her two sons.

Taffy Sinclair is perfectly gorgeous and totally stuck-up. Ask her rival Jana Morgan or anyone else in the sixth grade of Mark Twain Elementary. Once you meet Taffy, life will **never** be the same.

Don't Miss Any of the Terrific Taffy Sinclair Titles from Betsy Haynes!

Follow the adventures of Jana and the rest of **THE FABULOUS FIVE** in a new series by Betsy Haynes.

- -